THE CRACK AGREEMENT

FORMELY, ALL CRACKED UP

A Novel By

Madison Love

PUBLISHER'S NOTE

This book is a work of fiction. Names, characters, places, and
incidents either are products of the Author's imagination or are
used fictitiously. Any resemblance to actual events or locales or
persons, living or dead, is entirely coincidental. "The publisher
does not have any control over and does not assume any
responsibility for author or third-party Web sites or their
content."

Send inquiries to:

The Nibor Group
16405 Livingston Road, #164,
Accokeek, MD 20607

Printed in the United States of America.

DEDICATION

To every woman who feels that they are not worthy and do not truly love who they are, I am sorry for what you have endured. Please know that nothing and no one can define you. And that no surgery, weight loss, or man will work for you, if you don't love yourself first. When you look in the mirror, please love who you are and what God has created. Do not let other people or things deteriorate your self love. No matter what others say, it's important to know that you are beautiful and you are worthy.

My quest in life is to help women find self-love by letting them know that they are enough and to accept nothing less than their worth.

—Madison Love

ACKNOWLEDGMENTS

Special thanks go to my husband Jerry for the love and support he has provided me during this journey and throughout our life together. Thanks for your patience!

My sincere appreciation goes to my friend Natashia Brewer, Resonation Entertainment Group, for her support and encouragement by pushing me to continue on this journey and encouraging me to keep writing.

I am especially grateful to my mother, Annie Chambers, for offering her wisdom and guidance during our morning talks before getting the day started.

PROLOGUE

As the children lined up for recess, Lily made her way to the end of the line. She liked being the last in line, so she could avoid the banter from the other kids. Still, as she passed by, they began to chant, "Lily is a fatty… Lily is a fatty," continuously until they reached the playground. The teacher was so accustomed to the chant that she no longer disciplined them for teasing Lily. When the class made it to the playground, Lily found her favorite oak tree and sat under it. This was her normal routine on the days she had recess. She hated being called names; it made her very sad. Since her parents' death when she was two years old, she has been switched from foster home to foster home.

Nobody really understood what she was going through. Eating was the only way that she knew how to deal with the pain from being teased at school. She had no friends to keep her occupied, so she ate from the time she got home from school until she went to bed at night.

Meanwhile, Samantha dreaded going to a new school in the middle of the year. She did not want everyone staring at her when she was introduced as the new student. She wondered if they would call her names like "Miss Piggy" like they did at her old school. She had been called names so often that she would join in on the laughter when the kids called her names.

However, deep down inside she wished she were pretty like the other girls in her class who had the boys doing anything for them. She knew she would never be pretty and slim like them, but she always prayed it would happen.

The office had to process her transfer paperwork, and it took a long time. It was midday when she was finally enrolled. Since it was recess time, the teacher escorted her outside where the fifth graders from her third period class were playing. Samantha looked around to examine the scenery. A few boys were playing basketball on the court, while a couple of girls stood on the sideline whispering and giggling. Other children were running around playing tag and other games. As Samantha continued to look around the playground, she saw a girl sitting under a tree with her face in her hands. She immediately went over to the little girl and sat next to her.

"Hi, I'm Samantha, but you can call me Sam. Are you ok?"

Lily looked up in shock, because no one has ever talked nice to her before. She hesitantly responded to the kind stranger.

"I'm Lily, but you can call me Lil. Are you new here?"

"Yes, today is my first day at this school. I moved here from North Carolina. What's wrong?"

"The kids here are cruel, so beware," Lil replied.

"I had to deal with the same thing at my school in North Carolina. I'm not going to take it here, though."

Her confidence made Lil curious because she knew how horrible her classmates were.

There's no way the new girl was going to be able to handle them.

"What are you going to do?" Lil asked. "My mom told me to toughen up, and

don't let anyone call me names anymore," Samantha responded confidently.

"So, what are you going to do?"

"I don't know, but you can stick with me. I will protect you."

The bell rang indicating that it was time to go inside. From that point on, Samantha and Lil were joined at the hip. The bullies at school continuously picked on them, but they learned to cope with it together. After school, they would stop by the local café and have ice cream and french fries. They would sneak off during school to eat candy together during recess. They vowed to remain friends forever.

Little did they know that their friendship would be tested later, and they would experience the most difficult times in their life together.

As innocent kids, they didn't imagine that their desperation to be thin would send them on a journey of crime, lies, and deceit. Furthermore, the young friends were unable to foresee that they would endure so much pain and suffering together. Inevitably, their friendship progressed, and their future issues quickly approached.

INTRODUCTION

My best friend Lily, also known as Lil, has lost all respect for herself. Her addiction is out of control, which is the main reason why I've committed us to this rehabilitation facility. Lil's addiction is much worse than mine is; but, addiction is addiction, and it's the same illness no matter who does it more. I only say that Lil is addicted more than I am, because she has done things for crack that you would never think a person of her status would do. At least I kept that under control; I had no choice. I am what you call a functional addict. Lil is a non-functional addict. However, with my help, I made it seem as though she was functional. You see, our families have no clue that we are addicted to crack. I do believe they are suspicious of something, but I'm almost certain that they do not think that it's drugs. I've been working very hard to cover that up. They think we are going through menopause or some kind of mid-life crisis shit, because we suddenly began to go out partying. What they didn't know was that we were actually at hotels smoking crack.

We realized that our addiction had gotten out of hand, so we signed ourselves up for a rehabilitation program. Unfortunately, our program of choice is in Arizona. Therefore, we had to develop a plan to get there without raising our husbands' suspicions. Lil and I told them that we were flying to Arizona for a mini-vacation. I literally had to force Lil to go. This program is our last resort, and if it does not save us, I'm afraid of what may happen. I have maxed out all of my credit cards, and I was ready to sell me and my husband's jewelry before I made the decision to come here. On top of that, Lil's husband does not know that she has been fired from work due to not

4

coming in or frequently arriving five hours late. We work together, so they believed it. Between the job loss and dangerous encounters, I needed to get far away to clear my head and face my situation head on.

Although I don't currently accept that I am an addict, I'm hoping that I will walk away healed from the tragedies I faced during my addiction. After this program ends, I hope that my life will return to the life it once was when I was a little overweight but happy, healthy, and loved. My mother is watching our children, and they plan to go to Disney World. At least we don't have to worry about them while we're in here. Our husbands have been traveling a lot this summer, which is why they have not noticed the drastic things that have been happening with us. Oh, they've noticed the weight loss, but I don't think they've paid much attention to the behavioral patterns - at least my husband Ron doesn't seem to notice.

As I lay here reminiscing, the only thing I can think of is our lovemaking. Crack cocaine increases the sexual appetite. My husband made a comment one evening after we had just finished making love about me missing him a lot or learning new tricks from someone else. He was a little suspicious and wanted to know what was going on, because my performance as well as my endurance was well above the norm. I told him it was because he's been traveling so much this year that when he's away I realize how much I miss him. I convinced him that my sexual performance was my way of showing him. He jokingly said he should keep traveling if that's the reward he would get when he gets home. We made love all day that day. Shortly after that, I realized that if I didn't get myself healed, I could possibly lose my husband and the comfortable lifestyle that he has afforded me.

Lil does not want to be here. She enjoys smoking crack and has no desire to stop even after what happened to her. I'm hoping that she will realize how devastating it would be to her family if they find out what's she's been doing and who she's been doing it with for so long. Lil has been giving sexual favors to the drug man for crack because this addiction is an expensive habit. She has totally exhausted her bank account and now she's sleeping with the drug man to keep getting high. I endured hell the last two months while trying to keep her under control and maintain my addiction as well. I would smoke about two to six bags of crack a day. Lil would smoke about eight to twelve bags. My daily routine for the summer break was to wake up at 6:00 a.m., get the kids up, and take a shower. Then, after I would finish my shower, I would take a hit of crack. After that, I would get ready for work, fix the kids' breakfast, fix their lunch, drop them off at day camp, and arrive at work by 9:00 a.m.

At work, I was always busy doing something. One of the problems associated with smoking crack is anxiety in most people and paranoia in others. I suffered from both, and I thought everyone was talking negatively about me or was trying to get me fired. Therefore, I just stayed to myself. Lil worked in the Human Resources Department for the same company, so we would take lunch together most of the time. Of course, we fed our addictions during our lunch hour. We would leave work, park somewhere, and smoke more crack. We eventually had to stop going to the residential areas because we had a close call with the police. I'll never forget that afternoon. Lil had asked me to drive her SUV, and while we were smoking crack inside her vehicle, a police officer pulled up.

"Oh shit, a cop is coming!" I exclaimed and cranked up the engine to make the police officer think that we had just pulled up.

Lil quickly grabbed one of the water bottles that was resting in the cup holder and splashed some water on her face. The officer could not see her splashing the water because the windows were tinted, and he was parked on the opposite side of the street. He was walking towards the driver side of the vehicle. Meanwhile, Lil wiped her face gently with a napkin that she grabbed from the side pockets of the passenger side door. When the officer walked up, she began to act as if she'd been crying.

"Good afternoon, ladies."

"Good afternoon, sir," we both said in innocent, non-suspecting voices.

"I got a complaint that your car was parked in front of this house and suspicious activity was going on."

Lil continued her act.

"Officer," she said while pretending to sob, "I'm so sorry. I just needed someone to talk to, so my friend took me out of the office so that I would not cry there."

"Are you ok, Ma'am?"

"I just caught my husband with another man!" she cried hysterically. "Can you arrest him officer? Please arrest him! He has ruined my life!"

The officer was taken aback.

"I'm sorry, Ma'am, but if he didn't commit a crime, I can't arrest him."

"He slept with another man for God's sake! Isn't that a crime? It's in the bible that a man should not sleep with a man!"

"I'm sorry, but you ladies need to go to a better place to talk. The neighbors don't like people sitting in front of their houses."

"Yes Officer," I said and slowly pulled off.

That was a close call, but we managed to survive it as well as many others. I think the biggest obstacle for us to overcome is this treatment facility. In comparison to all of the drug deals gone wrong and the crack houses we've frequented, getting help seems to be the worst of all. We are not even certain of whether this treatment facility will be our ticket back to a life of peace and happiness. I always dreamed of being a size eight, and now that I'm there, the only thing I can think about is taking a quick hit. I could care less about how I look or whether I can fit into an outfit. On top of that, my husband notices the weight loss, but he likes me a little bigger. He says he likes a woman with meat on her bones. If he finds out the real reason behind me losing this weight, it would crush him.   He's the love of my life. *How could I be so stupid and risk losing such a good man and good life? God, I need you now!*

As I lay here leaden with regret in this dreary treatment facility, all I can think about is how foolish the idea of trying crack cocaine was. After seeing my crack addicted sister, Marie, at my annual Christmas dinner and how thin she was, my close friend Lily presented her plan on how we could get rid of the extra pounds we were both carrying. We were supposed to smoke crack for two months to curve our appetites. We figured that if we didn't eat during the crack diet, we would lose enough weight in two months to get into a size ten; although I preferred a size eight. It was an absolutely insane idea! Yes, it sounded great at the time, because we would have done anything to be thin. However, anyone in his or her right mind would have told Lily off, and the conversation would have been over.

Lilly Mae Robinson has been my best friend since elementary school. We talk on the phone at least twice a day. We see each other every day at work, and we always have brunch together on Saturday. We planned our pregnancies at the same time so our children could grow up together. Her children are very close with my children,

Ronda and Sam. Her daughter Michele is ten years old, and her son, Michael, Jr., is twelve years old. They all play sports together. Lil got married one month after I did so we could be in each other's wedding. Her husband, Michael, is very close to my husband, Ron.

Looking back, I know that Lil and I were not in our right minds. Throughout childhood, we both were always bullied and teased in school because of our weight. Deep down inside, we still were suffering from the abuse that we had to deal with back then. Therefore, the thought of being thin took over any logical thinking. What would make a person be so desperate that they would agree to experiment with illegal drugs as an attempt to being slim? If you analyze this from a psychological aspect, the answer would be *desperation.*

Lily and I lost the weight we wanted to lose by smoking crack, but we lost a whole lot more as well. The most important thing that I lost was my dignity and my best friend. Lily lost herself; she is not the same person that she was before our crack diet. I pray to God that I'm able to restore my life and Lil's back to the way it was before that evil substance decimated our souls.

***

It was sweltering outside, and I had just come in from my daily stroll around the courtyard at the treatment facility. I would usually walk around the tan-colored building three times each day; however, due to the heat, I only made it around once today. The building had a welcoming appeal to it. It resembled an old historic building from the 1940s, and it appeared as though it was restored to add a twentieth century flair to it. The gardens were filled with all sorts of beautiful flowers. Of the many flowers and colors, I was only familiar with a few - the   hydrangeas, hyacinth, and the peonies. They filled the air with a fresh and sweet scent. The way they were placed in the landscape looked like a portrait resembling a spring day. Since tulips are my favorite flower, I think the garden would have been perfect if it had some rows of purple and yellow tulips. As I gazed at the beautiful assortment of flowers, it reminded me of my desire to have a flower garden in my yard. I always wanted to step outside of my front door and clip flowers from my garden, so that I could have fresh flowers greet me as I entered my home each day. I made a mental note to pursue that dream when I finished with my treatment here.

I finished my therapy session for the day, met with my counselor, and then ate an early dinner with Lil. Both Lil and I had therapy sessions that included Behavioral, Psycho- education and Planning, Assertiveness, Relaxation, Functional Analysis, and Exposure Training. Today was the Psycho-education session where the instructor helped me with behaviors and contingencies that were maintaining my addiction. She also worked with me to create a plan to promote behavioral change. After dinner, I went back to my room, showered, and got into bed. Unfortunately, I was unable to sleep. All I could think of was my life, and I asked myself, *"How did I end up in here being treated for drug addiction? What if something happens to me?"*

You see, my husband wouldn't have even known where to find me, because he had no idea that I was there. I think about how much it would have hurt him if he actually knew what I'd done.

I could feel my heartbeats speed up as I imagined the pain my family would endure. I couldn't hurt them like that. I remember when Ron and I met and married. Shortly after our marriage, our children, Sam and Ronda were born. Our life was so beautiful. *How did I get here?* I can't help but think about how it all started…

CHAPTER 1

"Samantha Jane Love, will you please hurry up for God's sake!" Ron yelled angrily up the stairs at me.

I was upstairs in the bedroom putting on the last of twelve dresses that I had already tried on tonight. They were all strewn across the bed and all of them made me look huge. I had planned to hang them back up, but Ron was getting very irritable. He usually calls me by my full name when he's really pissed off.

"We're going to be late," he bellowed. "The party starts at ten o'clock, and that gives us just twenty minutes to get there."

Ron is a very punctual person. I can't recall the last time he ever arrived late at anything. His orgasms are even on time! The dress I'm wearing is a black satin dress with rhinestone spaghetti straps. The spaghetti straps are beautiful - although, it's unfortunate that no one will see them because I would not dare show my arms. They're too flabby and too big. Therefore, I will keep on a nice black jacket with the dress all night.

We're headed to the annual holiday party for Ron's company. I don't enjoy going to his company parties, because most of the women there are so shallow. The seating is assigned, and every year we get stuck at a table with Ron's business partners and their wives. The men would all head to the cigar room and leave the women at the table. As always, the entire conversation with the women was about themselves or the latest material things that they purchased or their husbands purchased for them. They never talk about their children, politics, world hunger, volunteerism, or anything worthwhile. It's always about the new car their husband just bought

10

for them or the five-carat diamond ring they just received. When I try to ask them about anything other than themselves, such as, the latest news event, they have responses like, "Oh my God, Samantha... Who has time to watch television or read the paper? I have to keep my spa appointments, darling."

It's brutal because I'm such an outcast. Only three of the women at the table have a job, and I'm one of them. The rest of them are all housewives, and they all have maids. I thought I would at least have something in common with the two employed ladies at the table, but I don't know which was worse - the housewives or the ladies with a job. The employed ladies have very high positions on their jobs. Since I am *only* an Executive Assistant, they would criticize and say, "Why do you bother to work? Your husband is doing very well?"

I would kindly respond, "I want to work. My children are in school, so I want something to do all day. Besides, my boss is very flexible with me."

I play along with them, but inside, I'm so humiliated. I mean let's be real... They're not *that* well off. Yes, their husbands make very good money just as mine does, but the cost of living in the Washington, DC area is *not* cheap. Therefore, I would consider everyone sitting here at this table with me as high upper class, but nowhere near multi-millionaire status. Furthermore, as I sat here listening to the various conversations, I noticed that they never have anything nice to say about any young lady who walked into the ballroom wearing larger than a size eight.

If she was even a half size larger, they would bellow out, "Oh my God, how can she be so big? She's going to lose her husband."

Those horrid words make the little self- esteem that I have left leave my body instantly. So while Ron is off networking with his fellow associates, smoking cigars, and drinking port wine, I'm stuck at the table sulking with *The Stepford Wives*, wishing I could take my size sixteen ass home to cry! That's why I hate these damn company events! *Why do I let these fake ass women bother me so much?* As they continued to criticize most of the other ladies in the ballroom, I excused myself from the table and went outside to call Lil. As I walked away from the table, they all began to laugh. I know they were laughing at me, because I was much bigger than the ladies they were just criticizing. I felt like I was in grade school all over again.

When I finally escaped the evil witches at my table, I talked with

Lil for about an hour. She had me laughing so hard, and I felt much better. When I returned to the party, Ron was back from his networking and he rescued me for the remainder of the night by keeping me by his side. We would dance, and then we would take a walk out on the terrace to cool off. When a slight breeze blew, I noticed that he had a rustic smell reeking from his clothing. It was from the cigar smoke that had absorbed into his suit during the length of time he spent in the cigar room. The smell of port wine was on his breath, and the two combined made him smell rather manly, similar to a leather smell. His scent made me imagine him on top of me with his beads of sweat dripping onto my face. I love a sweaty man!

We both were pretty buzzed. Ron switched from port wine to cognac. I'm a wine lady myself. It does it for me every time. After two glasses, I'm a little gaiety. Ron is a cognac man. When he is feeling really buzzed from the cognac he gets this kinky look on his face. When he looked at me when we arrived back at the table with *The Stepford Wives*, I knew it was time to go home. After we danced a little more and cooled off, we left the party and went home to make passionate love. I can't believe that he still has the ability to pull out new tricks during our lovemaking sessions. He turns me on so much, and I love him with all my heart. Although our chemistry is still as strong as ever before, I wonder if the ladies at the table are right. Will Ron leave me because I'm not the average size six woman? What if I continue to gain weight during our marriage? Will he be embarrassed to take me to his company parties? Does he hide the pictures of me that I placed in his office so nobody would know that he has an overweight wife? What am I saying? Those women have me doubting myself and lowering my self-esteem even more. I need to do something about this and not give them the control of how I feel about myself.

***

Ron and I have been married for fourteen years. We have two wonderful children, Ronda Bay Love and Samuel Christian Love. Ronda Bay Love is ten years old, and Samuel Christian Love (Sam) is twelve years old. Sam was conceived during the time when Ron and I became born again Christians. We joined a Baptist church in the neighborhood. We were baptized there and have been very active members ever since. Ronda Bay was conceived while Ron and I were away for a "got to get away from it all" weekend. We dropped Sam off with Ron's mother, "Grandma Love," and got in the car and drove until we were exhausted. We ended up somewhere in Maryland at a luxury hotel located east of the Chesapeake Bay.

After checking into the hotel and settling in the suite, we went for a walk outside right along the water's edge. We came across a big boulder and decided to take a seat there to watch the stars. As we sat in awe, the cool breeze brushed against our skin with such gentle movements. It was very romantic. Ron and I talked about how lucky we were that we found each other. He grabbed my hand and began to caress it. Using one finger at a time, he began rubbing my hand in a circular motion, as though he was trying to figure out the pattern of each of the wrinkles on my finger.

I bet if anyone ever asked him, he would be able to tell the direction of the wrinkles on my left pinky finger. He pays attention to every detail. That's why his love is so strong and so undeniable. He began to kiss me and caress me so much that I could not resist his touches any longer. He pulled me to my feet so that we could go to the suite, but the night was too beautiful. I wanted to stay there, so we made love right next to that boulder. That was the best lovemaking we ever shared - right at the edge of the Chesapeake Bay. Nine months later, Ronda Bay Love was born.

***

We reside in an upscale neighborhood in a tranquil gated community. Our country/colonial home is located on a lakefront property located in Ocean View, Maryland. Lily and her husband Michael live in the same community about five minutes from us. Ron is the Executive Vice President of Sales and Marketing for a Telecommunications company in downtown Washington, D.C. He has been with his company- RiverTel for ten years now. I love to visit his office and walk in to see Ronald J. Love engraved on a name tag on his door. It took a lot of work for him to get where he is today. He deserves it and so much more. I only use his full name, Ronald Jacob Love, when I'm furious with him, and that's not very often.

I work as an Executive Assistant, Personal Assistant (and anything else you want to throw into the pot) for the CEO/Founder of an advertising company. My boss, Daniel, is a royal pain in the ass, but I tolerate him because he allows me to leave early enough to transport my kids from one activity to the next and to make their games/events. I make decent money, but Ron is definitely the breadwinner of the household. I could not survive my current lifestyle without him. I only got this job because I needed something to do while the kids are in school. I did the volunteering thing for a year, but I came to realize that I just don't do other people's kids.

Some parents let their children run things, but I was raised by some very strict and firm parents. If I talked while they were speaking, I would get popped in the mouth, and Lord help us all, if I interfered in "grown folks" conversation. My mother would stop right in the middle of the conversation that she was having with her friend, grab me up by my shirt, and tell me to stay out of grown folks' business. I knew that I had better not repeat a word that I heard. I was so confused back then, because if they didn't want me in grown folks' conversation, then why talk around me. However, her point was well taken.

I was afraid to repeat anything I heard, because if Mama found out, she would make me pick my own switch for her to beat my behind. If I came in from picking my own switch and it was not big enough, she would go and get it herself. She would intentionally get the biggest one she could find. I swear, it was child abuse back then, but all parents did it. If you did something wrong at your friend's house, your friend's parents would beat you, call your mother, tell her what you did and that they beat you, and then when you got home, your mother or father would beat you again. It was rough, but that kind of discipline shaped me into the woman that I am today. Wait! Maybe that's *not* such a good thing! The current woman I am today has low self- esteem, and I am overweight. Maybe I should rethink this…

Nevertheless, I volunteered at my children's elementary school when they were seven and nine years old. Those were the worst days of my life. My kids went to private school from first to sixth grade. I put them in private school during their early grade school years because of what I endured in school at that age. They went to public school when they got a little older. Kids are just so damn disrespectful! I'm talking about little kids! They were only in second and fourth grade, and the things they'd say to an adult were unreal!

It took everything in me to tolerate those little brats. You see, if those were my children, they would not have teeth in their mouths. They know better. It's all about how you raise your children. What are these parents doing these days? They damn sure aren't raising their children. You can't be your child's friend; you have to be a parent first. Anyway, I had to give up the volunteering at the schools before I got convicted of murder. Besides, Sam and Ronda were pretty glad I stopped. They were sick of seeing their mom in their classrooms all of the time.

***

Ron and I met at a library in downtown DC. I was there doing some research for one of my previous bosses. The research consisted of me finding and documenting information on all companies who offered Voice over IP services at that time. I had my nose in a book, or maybe I should say I had the book in my nose. It was so close to my face that you would have thought I was trying to hide from someone. I didn't realize it then, but I needed glasses. Anyway, I had the book very close to my face trying to figure out a missing word on the page. Someone had torn a page in the book and it did not match up neatly with the remaining text.

While I was on my mission, Ron walked up to me and said, "Pardon me Ma'am… Are you finished with that book?"

I brought the book down from my face very slowly to look up at the rude individual. I intended to show them that I was very annoyed because they were interrupting me, but I was instantly astonished by the sight! There stood this beautiful brown ornament covered with chocolate-colored skin, brown eyes, and black fine hair with little waves throughout. He also had pretty white teeth. I thought to myself, *this gentleman definitely goes to the dentist every six months from the looks of his teeth*. They were pure white and straight. Most men don't go to the dentist. They avoid the doctor's office at all costs, so the dentist is surely out of the question.

"I'm afraid I'm still using it," I managed to say between mesmerizing thoughts.

"By the looks of it, you look like you've been *afraid* all night. Why are you hiding that beautiful face behind that book?" he asked.

"Well," I said very girlish like, "I wasn't aware that I was hiding."

He sat down next to me, and we talked for well over two hours. Upon leaving, we exchanged numbers and went about our merry way. When I left the library and got into my car, I thought to myself, *that guy is not going to call me. I'm not his type. He was just trying to make conversation. What does a guy like that want with a girl my size?* I balled his number up and tossed it in the ashtray of my sedan. I never expected to hear from him again.

The next day, Ron called me at home to see if I was available for brunch. I could not believe it. He actually called me the next day! It was a Saturday morning, and I woke up at about 7:00 a.m. I lived in a condominium in Georgetown, located in the District's West End just blocks away from Foggy Bottom and Dupont Circle. I love to wake up in the morning when the rest of the world is still asleep, it is so peaceful. If you were not a native of DC, then you would think it was impossible since many compare DC to New York. In some instances, some folks refer to DC as the mini New York. However, I beg to differ.

As I sat at my kitchen table, looking out the window and listening to the birds sing as the sun starts to rise, I got a sense of déjà vu. While sipping on my coffee and watching a few cars ride by, I felt like I had experienced that moment before. There was a yellow Porsche sitting at the red light, and a couple walking hand in hand, probably coming from a nightclub. I had seen the yellow Porsche and the couple before. *Was it in my dream or does déjà vu actually exist?* One would never know, I guess. Anyway, it's funny how a city like Washington, D.C. can seem so country-like at seven o'clock in the morning.

After enjoying the morning activities, I accepted Ron's invitation for brunch. He arrived at my condo at 11:30 a.m. to pick me up. When he rang the buzzer, I pushed "0" on my phone, which grants access to my building. Ron came up one flight to my condo. I was dressed in a khaki- colored linen dress and a pair of black stiletto heels; I was looking sharp. The dress hugged my curves in just the right areas. Although I do have extra weight on me, it is proportioned to my body. I have what most consider an hourglass shape. The dress that I was wearing was a size sixteen. That's considered plus size no matter where you go in the world, and it's considered fat by many standards.

Ron came in and I asked him to have a seat while I went to my bedroom to get my purse. Before returning to the living room, I picked up the phone and called Lil.

"Hey Lil," I whispered.

"Hey girl! I'm getting ready to get up. What time do you want to do brunch today?"

"Oh, that's one of the reasons why I'm calling."

"Why are you whispering?"

"You know that guy I told you about who I met at the library?"

"Yes, the one you said you know wouldn't call, but it was nice for a fine brother like that to show interest in you? What about him?"

"Well, he's here, and we are going to brunch."

"What! See, I told you he would call! Wait. Hold up, you are going to give up our girlfriend time for a guy you don't even know?"

"I promise I will make it up to you, Lil," I pleaded, as I walked to my bedroom window to look out at Ron's car.

I needed to give Lil his license plate number just in case I don't make it home. From the partially obstructed view, I was able to tell that he had Maryland license tags that had "Jus B U" on them. It was a black Sedan that looked like a Toyota Camry.

When I gave Lil the tag information, she laughed and said, "Just be you!" You have got to find out what the hell that means."

I laughed quietly and said, "I'll call you as soon as I get back."

I gently put the phone down so that Ron would not hear me hang it up. Then, I proceeded to brunch with the gorgeous guy who would become my future husband.

CHAPTER 2

When I came out of my room ready to go, I found Ron standing in front of my wall unit looking at photos of my friends and family.

"Who is the young lady in this picture with you?"

"That's my best friend Lily. She is like my sister," I replied.

Then, I showed him the other pictures of me with my mom and dad as well as the family picture with mom, dad, my two brothers, and my two sisters.

"You have a nice looking family. Where do you fall in birth order with your siblings?" he asked.

I picked up the pictured and pointed to each person as I listed our birth order.

"I am the youngest. John is the oldest. Then came Jimmy, Debra, Marie, and then me. We are all two years apart," I explained.

I am close with all of my siblings except for Marie. She and I used to be really close. We used to go shopping together shared each other's clothes, and told secrets to one another. That was until Marie started using crack cocaine, and she quickly went downhill. Marie was the best looking of all the girls. Debra and I used to hate for Marie to go with us to the local dances, because she would get all of the guys. When she turned one down, that's when they would look at us with interest. However, we didn't want her rejects!

Debra and I talk every Sunday. We are pretty close. She treats me like I'm a child, so I have to put her in her place every so often. She takes it humbly though, and we move on as if our disagreement never happened. Debra and Marie are still close. Debra has Marie's children, because Social Services took them away. This came after Marie left them at home for a week while she was out in the streets smoking crack. Marie's children, Jason (3) and Deirdre (5), are such wonderful children. I would have taken them in, but Debra does not have any children. Therefore, she jumped at the opportunity.

Marie used to be a big girl, or to be politically correct, she used to be a plus-sized woman. She gained the weight after she got married and had her children. She had the "brick house figure" that all the guys would go crazy over. Her husband, Robert, was always riding her back about losing the weight after her children were born.

He would call her names and humiliate her in front of people by saying things like, "Marie, I know you are not eating cake." She would be so embarrassed. There were plenty of incidents at our family holiday dinners where my brothers would kick him out of the house for talking to Marie the way he did. He would apologize to the family, saying it was the alcohol. Mom and Dad were torn apart about how Robert treated Marie. We always talked about it amongst ourselves, but never to Marie because she was in denial. We all felt that if he talked to Marie like that in front of us, we can imagine how he talked to her at home. Well, we eventually found out just how bad it was when Jason and Deirdre told us everything. We tried to get Marie to leave Robert, but she was defending everything he did to her. Eventually, Robert left her, and that is when she began her journey with smoking crack cocaine. She would go missing for months at a time. Heck, I wonder whether she plans on coming to my house next month for Christmas dinner.

***

When Ron and I arrived at the restaurant, we were shocked to see the line out the door. Ron said he had made reservations, but once we parked and got in, we still had to wait thirty minutes. So much for the reservations, they were useless. There was a live jazz band playing, and people were everywhere. We later found out that the Jazz band that was playing, *Smooth Sensations*, was one of the popular Jazz bands in the DC area. That explained why it was so crowded and why we had to wait so long with a reservation. The restaurant seemed like the hottest place to be on a Saturday afternoon.

We were finally seated at a table for two in a corner near the *Smooth Sensations* jazz band. The crackling from the fireplace, the flickering of the candles, and the movement of the musicians made me feel as though I was in a dream. My heart was in tune with every beat the band played. Ron and I ordered the buffet, which was to die for. There was an omelet bar, a waffle bar, and a host of any kind of breakfast foods that you could dream of having. If you did not see what you wanted on the bar, they would fix it for you in the kitchen. The service was superb. On top of that, Ron was quite the gentleman. He pulled my chair out for me to sit, took my jacket, and hung it up on the nearby coat rack. He even listened to me very intently. It was as though he was really interested in knowing me, rather than just getting into my panties like most of the guys I went out with over the last few months.

After we finished brunch, Ron suggested that we ride around to see some sights and continue our conversation. I was having such a good time that I barely let him finish suggesting it before I answered yes. I must admit, I was deeply enamored by this brother. He was well- groomed, very well-educated, a gentleman, and fine as hell. I kept telling myself, *Samantha, it's just a date and you know his type. It won't last. He doesn't like your type. You definitely won't be going home to meet his Mama!*

Well, it did last, and I did meet his Mama. We dated two years before Ron proposed to me. Although we had our ups and downs, we made it through. In the beginning, my insecurities got in the way. I just could not believe that a man like Ron would be faithful to me or that he wanted to be with me for as long as he had. I mean, I'm a good catch, but I'm the plus-size woman that wears a size 14/16. Every time Ron and I go out, I see many of the size 6 and 8 women looking at him in awe. Each time, I can't help but wonder if they are thinking *what the hell was he doing with Ms. Piggy!*

CHAPTER 3

For the majority of my adult years, I have been dieting. I have tried the Cabbage Soup Diet, Medifast, Weight Watchers, Jenny Craig, fasting, eating once a day, Dr. Phil's Ultimate Weight Loss Challenge, e-diets, extreme exercising, Metabolife, Oprah's Boot Camp, and a host of many more that I can't even remember. To my dismay, none of them were a long-term fix. Yes, I lost the weight, but it always seemed to slowly creep back to its rightful owner. So, here I am again trying to find that one miracle diet that will get me to a size 8 and keep me there for the remainder of my life.

Lil has been riding right next to me during this roller coaster with my weight. We have been there for each other through the good and bad times. You can say that we serve as each other's psychiatrist, counselor, healer, and motivator during our times of depression over our weight. In fact, we did all of those diets together, except for the Cabbage Soup Diet. Lil is not a big soup lover and refused to eat cabbage soup every day, all day. We are approximately the same size. The only difference is that she has larger breasts and would need a size 16 top and 14 bottom. I am the opposite; I would need a size 14 top and 16bottom. Most of the time we would shop together, buy the same outfits, and switch the tops and bottoms to fit our bodies. Other times, when we would shop alone, we would secretly switch the pieces of a suit or other two-piece outfit to the larger or smaller size, and pray that the sales associate would not look at the sizes. It worked most of the time. We realized that complimenting the sales associate on their hair or clothing worked every time, especially at the high-end department stores.

It seems that we have always talked about our weight. We ask each other every day about what we are wearing and whether or not we did our workout for the day. Sometimes, I call her in tears and start telling her that I'm sick and tired of being fat and that I'm feeling unattractive. She would ask if I am PMSing. I confirm her suspicion, and then, she informs me that she is also PMSing. Ten minutes later, she knocks on my door with ice cream. She would have each of our favorites - a pint of butter almond for me and a pint of cherry vanilla for herself. Then, we sit together eating the ice cream and whining about our weight, our husbands, and life in general. You know when it's that time of the month, everything makes you miserable no matter how great you're living or how healthy you are. You just feel like the whole world is against you. In your heart, you just know that they all hate you and think you are fat. While whining about our lives, we ate the entire pints of ice cream. As a result, we cried because we overindulged and felt fat and bloated! After we finished our crying session, we began talking about what we were getting our kids for Christmas. Sam and Michael, Jr. both want an Xbox system with about five games each. Ronda wants a karaoke machine, an iPad, and clothes. Michele wants roller skates, a skateboard, and clothes. She's a little bit of a tomboy, but Lil feels she will grow out of it. Plus, it keeps her active so she won't have the same weight problems Lil had when she was younger. Lil and I will go shopping next week to get the items on their lists. We have a couple of additional items we will get as well.

Lil and her family always come over for Christmas, because we go over to her house for Thanksgiving dinner every year. Her parents died in a car accident when she was young. Therefore, her grandmother who is now deceased raised her until she started grade school. When her Grandmother took ill and passed away, she was placed in foster homes. She gets a somber look on her face every time she talks about her life while in foster care. She said that some families really are only in it for the money and treated her really bad. She was the only child, so she doesn't have any family left. Her husband's family is large, so she has plenty of in-laws. When we got to her house last month on Thanksgiving, there were so many people there that it was unbelievable. There were plenty of cousins around for Michael Jr. and Michele to play with that day. Ronda and Sam always enjoy going over to Michael and Lil's house for Thanksgiving because of all of the excitement. Although we arrived there late after visiting our families first, the house was still full with guests and we had a great time as always.

Every year on Christmas Eve, Lil comes over, and we cook all of the food that can be cooked ahead of time. We usually start around 9:00 a.m. and finish around 9:00 p.m. We do a lot of cooking, but we have our bottles of wine and good conversation ready and waiting, so the time flies by. Since Christmas is two weeks away, we are looking forward to our day of cooking. Lil and I both have some new recipes to try this year. I suggested to Lil that we make a trial dish of the new recipes before Christmas day. She was against that idea.

"Child please, you know our folks eat anything. Just dress it up real pretty, and they will eat it - especially if they're drinking."

"Good point," I replied with a chuckle.

Lil was definitely right, so we will not be doing a test. However, I sure hope these recipes come out good.

***

Lil arrived at my house at 9:00 a.m. sharp on Christmas Eve with Michael Jr. and Michele trailing behind her. Michael Jr. took off up the stairs to Sam's room so they can play their video games. Michele found Ronda in her room talking on the phone. The kids are so roused up. All they have been talking about is Christmas day and what they plan on getting from Santa. At their age, I'm sure they know that Santa does not exist, but it's more fun to pretend that he does. Christmas is both of our families' favorite time of the year.

I had the coffee waiting when they arrived. Once Lil got settled, we sat down to enjoy our coffee before we started cooking. Meanwhile, we chatted about everything under the sun. Before we knew it, an hour had passed before we even began to cook. We made all of the desserts first.

"Sam, let's make the cannoli cake roll first.

It's from one of the new recipes."

"What's in this cake?" I asked as I skimmed the recipe. "Lil, this recipe takes twenty-three ingredients! We sure do need to start on this one now since it seems like it will take a lot of time."

Lil laughed at my reaction and took another sip of her coffee. That's why we should have taken that test run like I suggested a couple of weeks ago. She found the cannoli cake roll recipe online. Since we love the holiday season so much, we usually start searching for new recipes in October. The instructions for making the cannoli cake roll takes up two 8 ½ x 11 sheets of paper. That should give you an idea of how time consuming it is to make. Lil is famous for always trying unusual and exotic stuff. However, why would she pick a recipe that takes at least three hours to make? She's on her own with this one. She asked me to pick up the ingredients but I didn't know the recipe was so tedious.

Lil began her work on the cannoli roll while I began work on the other new dessert recipe - Kentucky Butter Cake. This cake is fairly easy. Most of its ingredients are already in the cupboard. It didn't take much time for me to whip this one up. When I finished with the butter cake, Lil was just halfway through with the cake roll. She was at the point in the recipe where she had to make the ricotta filling to go inside the cake. She had already baked the cake in a jellyroll pan and had it cooling on the rack. It may have been tedious, but I sure hope it tastes as good as it smells. After she spread the ricotta filing over the cake, she rolled it back up in a jellyroll and put the icing on it. Three hours and fifteen minutes later, the cake was complete. It looked really nice. When we serve it tomorrow, we will sprinkle it with shaved chocolate and chopped pistachios.

In addition to the two new cakes, we made six sweet potato pies, six pumpkin pies, one apple pie, one chocolate cake, one pineapple upside down cake, one pound cake, and one red velvet cake. That's just the desserts! According to the guest list, there will be approximately fifty-six people in attendance for Christmas dinner. That's only from those who RSVP'd. You know people always show up with some extra baggage. Last year, my brother came through the door and said, "This is my friend. You don't mind do you?"

I just forced a sweet smile and replied, "No, it's fine."

I wanted to say, *"Hell yeah I mind! You could have called me in advance to see if it was ok. Why would you ask me while you're standing at my door walking in? That's why I sent out the invitations and an RSVP number."* Our folks… what are you gonna do with them?

We started on the salads after we finished the desserts. We made potato salad, macaroni and tuna salad, plain pasta salad, seafood salad, chicken salad, and garden salad. After we finished making the salads, we moved on to the side dishes which included candied yams, collard greens, squash casserole, macaroni and cheese, corn soufflé, green bean casserole, and cabbage. By the time we finished all of side dishes, it was 9:00 p.m. We didn't even get to the meat, so we decided to cook the ham, beef brisket, salmon, and fried chicken in the morning. Ron and Michael Sr. usually deep-fry the turkeys about two hours before the guests arrive. Dinner starts at 3:00 p.m.

CHAPTER 4

On Christmas day, the kids woke Ron and me up around 3:00 a.m. They were so excited that we sprung to our feet and raced down the stairs with them, despite the exhaustion that consumed both of us. We wanted to see the look in their eyes when they opened their gifts. Ron had the camcorder rolling as Sam and Ronda opened all of their gifts. They were so happy to see that they got everything they had asked for plus a little more. Sam took over the camcorder while Ron and I opened our gifts. Ron was ecstatic with the gift I got for him. It was the new satellite radio he had been searching for over the last couple of months. It has been sold out and the retail stores were on back order. I had a few connections, and I used it to my advantage to purchase the radio. I'm glad I made his day.

Ron gave me the best gift ever, a beautifully wrapped purple and gold box. It was a diamond necklace with earrings to match, and it was beyond gorgeous. Sam and Ronda put their allowance together and gave Ron an iPod that he wanted to use while working out. They both gave me a smooth jazz collection which included twenty CDs and an iPod as well. I know Ron helped them buy the gifts just as I helped them buy his gifts. After we cleaned up the mess from the wrapping paper, we all went upstairs to get dressed for church. Lil and her family attended the sunrise service with us. It lasted for an hour and we were back home by 7:30 a.m.

Lil followed us home to help me cook all of the meat just as we had planned. We finished around noon, which gave her time to rest a little before she and the family came back for Christmas dinner. The guests began to arrive around 3:30 p.m. I said three o'clock on the invitation, but you know black folks ain't never on time. My parents, Paul and Ann Brown, who drove from South Carolina and Ron's parents, Jacob and Ella Love, were the first to arrive. Shortly after our parents arrived, the remainder of the guests seemed to trickle in one after the other. My sister Debra was the last to arrive. She had my sister Marie's children with her as well. They grew much taller since the last time I saw them, and they both looked just like Marie. I hope she is doing okay out there in the streets.

As I began to close the door, I felt a little resistance from the other side as if someone was trying to push it open. When I opened the door to see what the problem was, there was Marie standing there!

"What, you don't want me to come in?" she asked in a jokingly upset tone.

"Marie! Oh my God, it's you!" I exclaimed and hugged her tightly.

Her body felt thin and fragile. I chose not to mention it, because I wanted to enjoy my sister without our usual arguments.

"Yes Sis, it's me. Do you have room for one more?"

"Oh don't be silly, of course I do," I replied as I stepped aside to allow her to walk inside the house.

When Marie came in, everyone sort of paused for a moment, and then ran to greet her. It had been over a year since the family had seen her. Lil and I looked at each other and excused ourselves so that we could finish up in the kitchen.

"What happened to Marie?" Lil asked.

"I don't know, Lil, but she sure is skinny. I want to hold her down and feed her that entire turkey in there. She looks rough doesn't she?" I asked, thinking about how small Marie's body felt in my arms.

"Yeah, she does. Marie used to be kind of chunky. Now look at how small she is. Hell, if crack can keep you thin like that, I should give it a shot."

"Lil, you're crazy, girl."

"No, I'm not crazy. I'm desperate to be slim," Lil said without cracking a smile.

"Well, I'm not that desperate."

"Sam, who are you fooling? You have taken Fen Phen, Shaperite, and all those other drugs that had ephedrine in them. Now the FDA has pulled them off the market because they can kill people. So why is crack any different?"

"Because it's illegal! That's why, Lil! I'm not doing anything illegal. Yes, I said I would try anything to be slim, but I didn't say illegal. And, I can't even believe I'm discussing this with   you.

You can't be serious," I said, hoping that my friend hadn't lost her mind.

"Actually Sam, I am serious. After seeing how thin Marie is along with every other crack addict, the shit obviously works. I just want to try it one time to see if it curves my appetite."

Lil was obviously serious, because she was no longer basting the turkey. Instead, she was staring at me intensely. Nothing about her eyes said that she was joking. In fact, her eyes were glossy as if she was pleading for me to understand her.

"You're kidding me, right?"

"No, Sam, I'm not. Here's the deal, I will find a way to buy it. Just promise that you will try it with me. If it curves our appetite, we will do it for two months top. If it does not curve our appetite, we will quit immediately... Ok?"

I couldn't believe that Lil was saying this to me. Although what she was proposing was totally outrageous and stupid, I could not resist another extreme attempt at being thin. I guess when a person wants something so bad, they just want it, and thinking logically on how to get it is not part of the game. Nevertheless, I agreed, and Lil promised to get the crack in two weeks. Ron and Michael both will be out of town on that weekend. They're going on their annual Black Executives Moving Ahead (BEMA) conference in Las Vegas. Michael and Ron actually formed the BEMA organization. It went from ten members the first year to well over two-hundred fifty current members. I'm proud of what they've accomplished.

Lil and I went back into the dining room where we found Marie and Debra talking. We looked at each other, and Lil winked at me before going to sit next to her husband. The food was set up buffet-style, and there was practically no one in line. Everyone had their plates in hand and they were chowing down. Lil joined me while I was at the buffet.

"Are you still in Sam?"

"Lil, I said ok, but I'm still a little uneasy about it. It better work, you hear me?"

"Trust me, it will."

"Ok. Let's drop the subject until tomorrow.

I don't want anyone to hear us."

I fixed my plate and went into the dining room to sit with my parents and in-laws. Lil did not mention any more about our plan that evening. However, she did manage to get Marie all by herself. They were engrossed in a conversation over in the corner near the fireplace. I thought to myself, *what's Lil up to now?* I left her alone and continued eating my dinner with my family. The food was delicious. Lil and I outdid ourselves. I must admit that this was the best Christmas dinner ever. There was actually no food left to clean up. The family ate it all. Many went back a third and fourth time. That's a given on Christmas day, but I did want to have leftovers for dinner tomorrow. On the bright side, at least there was not much cleaning up to do.

Everyone had left by 9:00 p.m. I cleaned up the kitchen. Lil was going to stay and help, but I insisted that she go home with her family. I was in bed within thirty minutes. Ron was sound asleep when I entered our bedroom. He woke up when he heard the shower going. When I finished showering, I came out of the bathroom to a fully erect husband waiting for me. I saw Ron drink at least three glasses of cognac, but I'm pretty sure he consumed well over four. I knew he was lit up when he began to go around to the guests shouting, "Tis the season," and clicking his glass with theirs.

"You didn't think I was going to forget to give you some of this sweet chocolate now did you?"

I was so tired, but I knew my man was horny; so I went along with him.

"Oh no baby. I've been thinking about your sweet chocolate all day," I said sexily as I dropped my bathrobe and exposed my naked body.

"Then, come over here with your sexy ass and talk to *Rocky*. He misses you."

I got on top of my husband and slowly kissed him on his forehead. I then moved down to his neck and slowly kissed and licked him until I got to his midsection. He was hard as a rock and waiting for me to ride him. I caressed *Rocky* slowly with my mouth. Ron was moaning and groaning so sensually that it instantly turned me on. I guided *Rocky* inside me, and within minutes, we both were in sync with each other.

When Ron and I have sex, we always create a *taboo* scene and speak it aloud during our lovemaking to keep the excitement in our relationship. Tonight, as I was riding him, he began with his story…

"Ok baby, ride that thang. You know my wife is going to be home soon, so you better hurry and ride it good."

"Oh Ron, I don't want to rush this good loving. Please let me take it nice and slow. It's so good," I begged.

"Oh baby… You have to hurry. My wife will be home in a minute. Hurry… I want you to come with me," he moaned.

We grinded each other as if it was the last day on earth. When we both climaxed together, it was like a huge explosion. We yelled, screamed, and called on Jesus so many times that it was sinful.

"That was amazing," Ron managed to say between breaths.

"Yes it was baby, but I have a bone to pick with you."

"What's that?"

"What's up with that little fantasy? Was I the hired help or your mistress?"

"You were the hired help."

"You're sick, but I love it!" I laughed and playfully hit him with a pillow.

Ronda and Sam spent the night over Lil's house so we did not have to worry about them hearing us. We made love once more, and then fell fast asleep.

CHAPTER 5

The day that had me nervous since Christmas finally arrived. Ron and Michael left for their annual BEMA conference in Las Vegas. Lil had been on a mission to get started on this crack experience. I had done some research on the internet, and what I read about crack cocaine was startling. I was searching for ways to smoke crack, but all I found was rehab groups and the effects of crack cocaine. Every web page informed me of how you can become addicted to it instantly. However, I know that won't happen to me, because I am already aware of its effects. Therefore, I will just use it to curve my appetite for two months, no more. Marie was not an educated consumer before she began using crack. Not to mention, she used it because she was lonely and depressed after her husband left her. Crack uplifted her mood. I am already uplifted, I just need to lose thirty pounds, and I will be satisfied.

Michael Jr., Michele, Ronda, and Sam are all at a camping trip with the young teen's organization. Lil will be arriving at six o'clock this evening. She has to go and pick up the crack from Melvin, a longtime friend of hers. He's always had a crush on her. She asked him if he could pick it up for her. Turns out, he sells it part time. Lil told him it was for a friend of hers who is a high profile lawyer and does not want anyone to know what she is doing, and he fell for it. So we have our connection. When Lil met up with Melvin, she made small talk with him for a while, and then asked him nonchalantly, "How do people smoke this stuff anyway?" He told her that most people used a pipe but when a pipe isn't available, they use a beer or soda can. That peaked Lil's interest. Melvin explained to her how it worked.

She left his house after an hour, and then stopped at the convenient store to purchase a six- pack of soda, a pack of cigarettes, a candle lighter, and an ashtray. The sales guy looked at her very suspiciously as though he knew what she was up to. When she arrived at my house, we headed to the guest room upstairs. Lil explained how we were supposed to smoke it on the soda can. She went to the bathroom and poured the soda out of two cans into the toilet. Then, she held the can horizontally, crushed it in the center, and punched two holes where the folds of the can were. After that, she lit a cigarette and let it burn. She explained to me that we needed the ashes from the cigarettes so that the crack can rest on top of them and not burn the can. We would inhale the crack from the opening in the soda can. After she let three cigarettes burn, she broke off two pieces of the crack cocaine. She prepared my can first by putting the ashes on top where the holes were, and then she placed the piece of crack cocaine on top of the ashes. She picked up the lighter and told me to put my mouth on the can where we would normally drink from and then inhale. I told her I would wait, because we were going to do it together. She prepared her can the same way, but we still couldn't start at the same time since we only had one lighter. So I ran downstairs to the family room to get the lighter I used for my candles. When I returned to the guest room, we both put the cans to our mouths, and Lil told me the plan.

"Ok Samantha… Are you ready? I'm going to count to three, and all you do is inhale for maybe five seconds, and then exhale. One… two… three… Go!"

We both lit up the piece of crack cocaine that was resting on top of the ashes on our can. It made a crackling sound similar to the sound of wood burning in a fireplace but on a smaller scale. Instantly, the smoke came through the can and into my mouth. I inhaled as instructed, and then exhaled. I immediately felt a calming, soothing high. It was like an out-of-body experience, it was amazing! I felt as if I went into another world and floated so freely. I watched Lil as the feeling hit her.

"Oh my God! This feels so good! Samantha, do you feel what I'm feeling?"

"Yes Lil… Yes."

We took more hits from our crack until it was gone. Lil began to talk about everything. She talked about how good she felt, her kids, her husband, and her childhood. I wanted her to shut the hell up so I could continue to enjoy that exotic feeling. She finally settled down and began to pace the floor.

"What's wrong, Lil?"

"Oh nothing, I just want to make sure no one is coming, that's all."

After Lil checked the window to ensure that no one was outside, we put more crack on our cans, lit it, and inhaled. We did this over and over until it all was gone. Each time we put more crack on our cans and smoked it, Lil became more and more paranoid. She kept getting up, looking out the window, and going down the hall to check to see if someone was coming. That's the effect the crack had on her, it made her very paranoid. I noticed that I was sweating profusely and very nervous. Still, all could think of was that first hit and how pleasurable it made me feel. After we finished the last piece of crack, we laid around in the guest room and enjoyed the feeling. Lil continued to ramble on about everything, and I just laid around and watched the sun go down. Before we knew it, it was two o'clock in the morning, and we wanted more crack. I must admit, it does curve the appetite. We hadn't eaten anything since we started, and eating was the furthest from our minds. We just wanted to get high. That first hit of that crack cocaine was so amazing that I had to experience it again. Lil also wanted to experience it again, so she called Melvin to see if he had more crack. He answered his phone on the first ring. "Hi Melvin."

"Who is this?" "It's Lily."

"Oh, hello Lily. What's up with you calling me so late?"

"I know... I hate to be calling you so late, but my source asked me to get her some more. Can you handle that?"

"How much does she need?"

"She didn't say, but I would guess enough so that I don't have my ass out here in the middle of the night for her again."

"Ok, that would be an eight."

"What's an eight and how much does it cost?"

"An eight is twelve rocks. The cost is $200." "OK, I will be there in ten minutes."

"I fooled him! He's giving us an eight. It costs $200."

"Why so much?"

"It's twelve of the $20 rocks like we just smoked. I bought two rocks earlier and that was $40. This should last us for a while. I don't want Melvin to get any suspicion that it's me smoking it. You drive, Samantha. I feel like someone is following us."

"Girl, no one is following us…"

Just as I was getting ready to tell Lil to chill, my cell phone rang. It was Ron.

"Shit Lil, it's Ron. What do I tell him?" "Tell him we went to *The Late Nite Sax Lounge,* and we're headed home now."

"Hello."

"Sam."

"Hey baby. How are you?"

"I'm worried. Where the hell have you been all day, Samantha Jane Love? I've been calling you all day and on your cell since 8 p.m. What the hell is going on?" Ron asked in a worried yet forceful tone.

"Oh baby I'm sorry. Lil and I left the house around eight. We went to *The Late Nite Sax Lounge.* As a matter of fact, we are just headed home now."

"Where are the kids?"

Just as I began to answer, Lil's phone rang.

It was Michael, and Lil answered. "Hi honey."

"Lil, baby, where are you?"

"Samantha and I are just leaving *The Late Nite Sax Lounge.*"

"Oh, you went out without me huh? Don't be giving away my good loving… You hear me?"

Michael scolded playfully

"Oh baby… Don't you worry. Can't nobody take this from you."

"That's my girl."

"When will you be home?" Lil asked.

"The same time I told you before I left, and the same time I told you a week before that… Friday evening."

"You mean I still have to wait six days before I see the love of my life?"

"I'm afraid so."

"Ok, just hurry. I miss you baby."

"I miss you, too. Hurry and get home. It's too late for you two beauties to be out by yourselves."

"I think I will stay with Samantha tonight since the kids are gone to the camp. We can keep each other company. They won't be home until Monday morning. So I will stay with Samantha tomorrow night, too."

"OK baby. I will call you at Samantha's in the morning. Love you."

"Love you, too."

Michael was nice and calm, while Ron was hysterical. After Lil hung up with Michael, she looked over at me, and then covered her ears. Ron was yelling at the top of his lungs.

"I'm sorry baby, I didn't hear the phone," I pleaded.

Lil took the phone from my hand and said, "Hey, hey... What's with all the yelling? We left your house at eight o'clock and went to the club. Now we are on our way back to your house... By the way, I'm spending the night since the kids are gone. Sorry, I didn't mean to get you upset with Samantha."

Ron calmed down. Lil and Ron always had a relationship where they could talk to each other about anything. When he's upset with me, he would go to Lil; and when I'm upset with him, Lil would go to Ron and explain my point. He listened to her, but sometimes he wouldn't listen to me. Therefore, she would act as the mediator. Lil gave the phone back to me, and Ron was much more civil.

"Baby, I'm sorry. I was just worried and a little jealous, too."

"Jealous for what? Nobody wants this fat lady but you," I said softly.

"Don't start with the fat stuff again. You are not fat - just thick like I like it."

"Whatever... I love you baby. See you when you get home."

"I'm serious. I like you just the way you are. Now, hurry and get home. Call me when you get in so that I can rest easy tonight," he said in a much sweeter tone than he used at the start of the call.

"I will."

"Goodbye."

***

When we arrived on Melvin's street, I pulled over and parked the SUV on the side of the street. I got in the back seat and laid down so he would not see me. Lil got into the driver's seat and pulled into his driveway. I grabbed a blanket from the floor of the backseat and put it over me. Just   in case Melvin walked Lil to her car, maybe he would think it was just a blanket laid back there. I laughed to myself because I am not a small woman; therefore, anyone in their right mind would be able to figure out that a body was laying in the back seat. Although the windows were tinted, if someone was standing right next to the car, they would be able to see inside. To help conceal me a little more, I put the bags that were also on the floor on top of me. Lil went in and came back out about five minutes later. Melvin stood at the door and watched her as she pulled off. I did not sit up or say a word until we were out of his neighborhood.

"Did you get it?" I asked in a whisper as if he could hear me.

"Yep," Lil replied, and off we went for a second dose of crack.

CHAPTER 6

Lil and I arrived back at my house around 2:40 a.m. We called our husbands to let them know that we made it home safely. Then, we went upstairs to the guest room and started our quest to find that sensual feeling we got from our first high. Out of the twelve packs of crack cocaine, we had smoked only two packs so far, we were high as hell. It affects everyone differently. I did suffer from a little paranoia, but Lil kept thinking someone was after her. She was constantly opening the curtains, peeping out of the window, closing them again, running down the hall into the bathroom, and shutting the door. Watching her and how extreme she got with the paranoia ruined my high, so I just closed my eyes and enjoyed the ride.

I could feel my heart racing inside my chest. It was more noticeable than ever before. Therefore, I placed my hand on my chest to count the number of times my heart would beat within a minute. I could not keep track. I guess it was partly because I was so stoned that I couldn't focus long enough to keep count. Suddenly, I remembered the article I read about crack cocaine on the web before Lil and I got ourselves into this shit. It stated that, "Besides the feeling of getting high, there are many other common effects that you can get from smoking crack. They include increased heart rate, increased blood pressure, feeling dehydrated, increased alertness, intense anxiety, increased sex drive, paranoia, and sweating." Again, I thought to myself *why would someone in their right mind take such a risk with their life.*

I began to freak out when I thought about another article I read. That article was about the things that could happen when people smoked crack. The article stated that, "If you have not been taking care of your health, there is a good chance of you "doing the chicken." This is actually a blackout or type of seizure. There is also a chance of your heart stopping. This happens when you smoke a lot of crack, especially if you are stressed out or overtired, don't have much food or liquid in your system, or just generally have not been taking care of yourself." *There is a chance of your heart stopping.* This phrase kept playing over and over in my mind, and I began to hyperventilate. I was freaking out. As I began gasping for air, Lil was coming back into the room after running down the hall to make sure no one was in the house for the eighth time tonight.

"Samantha, what's wrong?" she asked frantically.

"Lil, I'm dying. I can't breathe. The article said my heart could stop. I knew I shouldn't have done this shit. Help me Lil! I'm dying!" I pleaded hysterically.

"What are you talking about, Samantha?

What article? Slow down, take a deep breath!"

I took the deep breaths as instructed. My heart was beating out of control.

"Feel my heart, Lil. I'm scared."

"Girl, your heart is beating so fast, 'cause you're sitting your ass over there thinking of some stupid shit you read."

"It's not stupid, Lil. It's the truth."

"Yeah, ok. Where did you read this article?" "On the internet."

"On the internet? Now you know that there is a lot of junk out there on the internet. Granted we both know that crack can be addictive, but it's up to us to keep ourselves under control. Now get up and walk it off, and stop thinking of negative shit. Ok?"

My heartbeats did begin to slow down. I was still high as hell, but my paranoia of dying subsided quickly. As I began to relax, I closed my eyes and went to a heavenly place. It was a place where lilac sand covered a secluded island. I was sitting underneath a palm tree with a glass of Cabernet Sauvignon. I had on a knee-length white peasant skirt and a halter-top. I was a size ten with a killer body. My caramel skin was smooth and had no signs of aging or cellulite. The wind was blowing through my jet-black wavy hair, and I would run my hands through it every now and again. I had lavender sparkles throughout my hair as a result of me lying on the sand to evenly tan my skin when the sun was shining. It was a beautiful place. I wanted to stay there forever. I suddenly came back to reality when I heard the phone ring. I ran into my bedroom to get the phone. I didn't want to miss any calls and go through the drama that Ron had put me through earlier this morning when he could not get in touch with me.

"Hello?"

"Hi Mommy." It was Ronda calling from camp.

"Hi sweetheart. Are you having a goodtime?"

"Yes! Mom you would not believe what I did."

Ronda went into her explanation about her hiking trip and how she climbed the ropes and beat all the boys up the rope first. She did not stop once for a breath. After she finished, she put Sam on the phone. As he talked to me about the good time he was having, Ronda was in the background yelling, "Sam's got a girlfriend."

"Shut up, Ronda."

"Sam, don't tell your sister to shut up." "Sorry mom. She talks too much."

"So tell me Sam… Did you meet somebody?"

"Mom!"

"Ok, Ok… I will butt out… Is she cute?" "Mom! I gotta go," Sam said with a pout and gave the phone to Michele.

I took the phone to the guest room and gave it to Lil. I mouthed to her before she got on the phone that it was Michele. Lil cleared her throat so that she would not sound so groggy on the phone. I noticed that crack really messes with your throat and makes you sound as though you have a frog in it. While Lil was talking with her children, I went downstairs to fix something to eat. We had not eaten anything since yesterday afternoon. I fixed us a ham and cheese sandwich with some chips. Then, I went to the wine cellar and grabbed a bottle of Pinot Grigio from the "everyday wine" section of the cellar.

We sat at the kitchen table and consumed our sandwiches as if someone was going to take them from us. We were so anxious to get back to getting high. As I took a bite from my sandwich, I watched Lil intently as she voraciously took large bites out of her sandwich. Her eyes looked as though they were ready to bulge out of her head as I poured the wine into our glasses. It's funny because Lil and I usually are very unreserved whenever we sit together. However, for some reason, we had nothing to say to each other at that particular moment. All we were thinking of was finishing our sandwiches so that we can go get high again. It's like we were afraid one was going to smoke more than the other. We made it back up to the guest room and smoked crack for the remainder of the night. We did not stop until three o'clock the next morning. We only stopped then because we had smoked an entire eight ball, and we were all out. We had to pick the kids up at one o'clock in the afternoon, so that gave us time to get some sleep. Still, all we could think about was getting more crack.

"You want to get some more, Lil?" I asked. "I was just thinking that, but how am I going to convince Melvin that I'm not the one who is smoking the crack? I just got some from him the other day."

"Well, don't go to Melvin. Let's go somewhere else."

"What do you mean somewhere else? The only other place is the street, and that is very risky. I'm not going to the hood to buy any crack, Samantha. Girl, you must have lost your damn mind."

"I remember when Debra and I went to look for Marie a couple of years ago, we went into the drug district downtown."

"You mean the hood downtown. You can't be serious, Sam?"

"Well, it's either downtown or Melvin, Lil.
Which will it be?"

"I guess it will be downtown because, if Melvin has any inkling that it's me smoking these drugs, he would probably turn me in to Michael." Instead of going to bed as planned, we jumped in Lil's SUV and headed for downtown SE Washington, DC. It's approximately twenty-five minutes from my home in Ocean View, MD. When we arrived on the street where I once visited in search of my crack addicted sister years ago, there were people out as if it was one o'clock in the afternoon. As we drove down the street, two guys approached our car.

"Whatcha looking for? I got that rock," he volunteered as if he knew what we needed.

Lil instructed the guy to give her four bags. She handed him the eighty dollars. He put the rocks in her hand, and she drove off. The rocks were separated into four clear plastic bags. Each rock was a little larger than a dime. We didn't pull the crack out until we got back to my house. Lil gave me two bags, and she kept two as we hurried up to the guest room. When I opened my bag, a pleasant fragrance seeped from it. The crack I smoked previously did not have a smell as fragrant as this. As I tried to break a piece off to put on my can, I noticed that the texture was also different. I put the crack up to my nose to get a better smell, and it smelled like soap!

"Lil, I think we've been scammed."

Lil had not opened her bags yet. She was busy preparing her can with ashes from the cigarettes she had burning in the ashtray. I handed one of my bags to her, and she smelled the rock that was inside.

"Fuck! That motherfucker sold us some damn soap. I can't believe this shit, Samantha!"

Lil was furious. She checked the other three bags, and they were all soap as well. We sat there for a while in utter silence. It was a bit of a disappointment, but there was no way we were going back out there.

"I guess we will have to go to Melvin," Lil said with a sigh of disappointment.

"I know, Lil, but it's too late now. We need to leave soon to go and get the kids."

We agreed to wait on our third high. Meanwhile, we went downstairs and finished off the wine and laid on the couch until we fell asleep.

CHAPTER 7

I was in the middle of a dream and loud banging on the front door woke me up. It seemed to get louder and louder with each knock. Suddenly, I heard voices.

"Mom! Mom!" I jumped up.

"Oh my God, Lil! It's the kids!"

When I ran to the door and swung it open, Mrs. Harris, the Camp Organizer, was standing on the front porch with the kids.

"Oh, I am so sorry. Please come in."

Mrs. Harris entered the house, and I noticed her looking around to see if she could find a reason to justify why I didn't make it to pick up my children. Ronda ran to me and gave me a big hug.

"Where were you, mom? Why didn't you come and get us?" Ronda asked.

"I'm so sorry. I must have slept through the alarm."

Mrs. Harris was very angry. She told me that I was on a warning, and if I failed to pick up the children again without calling or making prior arrangements, they would be banned from all future trips. The kids were so upset. Ronda ran up the stairs to her room and slammed the door. Sam did the same, but instead of running up the stairs, he stomped very hard on each step until he reached the top. Then, he continued as he made his journey down the hall to his room. Michael and Michele went to Lil and sat next to her on the sofa. There was nothing I could say to Ronda and Sam about their behavior right now. Under normal circumstances, that behavior would not have been allowed, but how could I reprimand them? I missed going to pick them up because I had been up smoking crack all night When I finally went to sleep, I slept past the alarm. I felt so awful and low.

Lil was answering many questions from Michael and Michele about why she looked so tired and why she didn't come and pick them up. She gathered her things, and she and the kids went home. As I walked them to the door, I suddenly remembered that we had our remnants from our crack experiment in the guest room. I hugged Lil and told her that I would call her later. Then, I dashed up the stairs to the guest room and put the cigarettes, soda cans, and the fake crack in a trash bag. I sprayed air freshener in the room to get rid of the lingering smell of cigarette smoke. Once I finished with the guest room, I turned the knob to Sam's bedroom to enter and make peace. Sam's room was just like most boys' rooms. There was stuff everywhere. He was supposed to clean it before going on the trip with the camp, but we were running late. Therefore, I instructed him to do it when he got back. I joined him on his bed and attempted to smooth things over with him.

"I know mommy messed up today. I'm so sorry, Sam. I was tired so I decided to take a nap, and I slept right through the alarm."

"We were the only kids whose parents didn't show mom. It was so embarrassing. The other kids were laughing at us."

"That had to be awful, huh?" "What do you think, Mom?!"

"I know… I know… That was a stupid question. Will you forgive your old forgetful mom?"

"Yeah, I guess so."

I went through the same routine with Ronda, but she was more dramatic and hysterical. However, the same outcome was achieved. I received forgiveness from both of my children. After that, we went to rent a movie from the new video rental store down the street from our home. We each picked a movie and played a game where we put the movies in a bag. We each would get a chance to pick a movie out of the bag when we got home. Whichever movie was picked twice, that would be the movie we would watch first. We would do the same with the following two movies. Once we picked the movie that would be watched second, we knew the last movie to watch as well. Sam won the first go around because his movie, *Drumline*, was the one that was selected from the bag twice. *Save the Last* Dance, Ronda's movie, was second. My movie, *Forest Gump*, was last. We enjoyed snacks while we watched the first two movies. When we went to put in my movie, I heard the garage door.

"Your daddy is home," I told the kids.

"Daddy's home!" screamed Ronda as she ran to the door. "Hi Daddy!"

"Hi Sweetie. How was camp?" Ron asked while bending down to hug Ronda.

"What's up, Dad?" Sam said as he gave Ron a high-five.

"Hey son. How are you?"

After Ron caught up with the kids about their trip, he came over to kiss me. I could tell from the look on his face that he was angry with me for not picking them up from camp. He didn't mention it because the kids were there, but I would definitely hear when we got in to bed. We ate dinner and attempted to watch *Forest Gump,* but everyone was dozing about twenty minutes into the movie. I made Sam and Ronda go up and get in the bed. Ron went upstairs to take a shower. While he was upstairs, I cleaned the kitchen and mentally prepared myself for his disapproval of me leaving the kids at camp.

When I entered the bedroom, Ron was still in the bathroom. He had finished his shower and was brushing his teeth. I removed my clothes and placed them in the hamper located in the walk-in closet next to the bathroom. I entered the bathroom and headed towards my side, but before I got there, Ron grabbed me and pulled me to him. He kissed me passionately, and I began to release the tension and guilt that I felt from leaving my children. I didn't understand why he was not angry. Ron is very protective about his family, and I just knew that he would be furious over this incident.

I took my shower, and then Ron and I made love. Our lovemaking was not as passionate and pleasurable, though. I could tell he had something on his mind. I guess he wanted to release some tension before addressing the issue with the kids, because frankly, he was very selfish. I didn't even have an orgasm. It was so quick, and he didn't even apologize. Immediately after he finished, he rolled over to face me so that he was looking directly in my eyes. When he does that, he is really pissed. It only lasted for a second or two before he went on his rant. He was so furious that he sat up in bed and began to yell, scream, and point fingers while making all sorts of gestures with his hands.

"So tell me, Samantha. What happened with you picking up the kids?"

"I don't know, baby. I set the alarm, but it didn't go off. Therefore, I slept right past the time. When Mrs. Harris knocked on the door with the kids, I was so embarrassed."

"You mean she had to bring the kids here? I thought you just showed up to pick them up late after all the kids were gone. But, hell, you didn't show up at all, and Mrs. Harris had to bring them to you? What the fuck was going on Samantha? What the fuck were you thinking? You don't answer the fucking phone when I call. I can't get in touch with you at all, and then I find out that you left my goddamn kids sitting, waiting for their parents to pick them up, and you never show. This is fucked up, and I'm pissed off about it. I want some answers now!"

"I'm sorry. I really don't know how I slept past the alarm."

"I don't know how either! You are up at the crack of dawn every goddamn morning! At   least when I'm home you are. Maybe you were out with your lover. Is that it Samantha? That's why you wouldn't answer the phone isn't it? I'm so pissed off with you right now. I gotta go."

Ron got up from the bed, got dressed, and left the house. Once I knew the coast was clear, I went to check on the kids to make sure they were asleep and didn't hear Ron screaming at the top of his voice. I hope when he gets back he is much calmer so that I can talk with him. I called Lil, and Michael had arrived home as well. Lil had told her kids not to mention anything to Michael about the incident. I told Lil that even if they didn't say anything, Ron would say something to Michael Sr.

"Shit, I forgot about that. I need to think of a way to mention it to Michael Sr. before he finds out from Ron."

"Well you better do it quickly, because Ron is so pissed off with me that he just left here. I don't know where he went, but I suspect he may show up at your place."

"Damn Sam. Let me go take care of it now.

I'll call you back when I'm done."

"OK. You make sure you call me back."

***

Lil called me back about an hour later. She said that she went into the family room where her husband was sitting in his favorite chair reading the paper. She sat on the loveseat so that she could face him directly. He looked up from the paper and smiled at her, and then went back to reading.

"Honey, I forgot to tell you something stupid I did while you were out of town. I forgot to pick the kids up from camp, and Mrs. Harris had to bring them home. She actually dropped them off at Sam's house because you know I spent the night there."

Michael slowly put the paper down and looked at Lily for what seemed like hours, but it was really only a few seconds.

"Samantha forgot to get her kids as well?" "Yes."

"That's interesting. You both forgot about your children."

"So tell me this, Lily. How did both of you forget about your children and not show up to pick them up at all?"

"We went to bed late that night. We were up watching movies and drinking wine, and we slept right past the alarm. Sam did set the alarm."

Michael's jaw began to twitch, which only happens when he is worried or upset. He began to tell Lily about how irresponsible she was, but the doorbell rang. Michael got up to answer it, and it was Ron. Both men left the house together about ten minutes after Ron arrived. As soon as they left, Lil called me to let me know that the men were gone together.

"They're on to us, Lil. We have to play it cool and get the suspicion off of us."

"Just don't do anything stupid and keep your cool. We can't go and get any more stuff yet, and starting now, we will not talk about it on the phone. We don't know if they are secretly tapping the phones, so it's better to be safe than sorry," I replied.

We talked on the phone for another thirty minutes wondering where our husbands were. We were being very careful not to mention our recent experience over the last couple of days. Ron arrived home at ten o'clock. Sam and Ronda were already asleep. I was in bed but could not sleep because I was worried about him being pissed off with me. Hell, I was pissed off with myself. How did I let Lil talk me into messing around with drugs like that? I couldn't even stop thinking about when we would be able to get more. I felt guilty, but at the same time, I wanted more. I just couldn't let my family find out about our secret. Ron walked into the bedroom and did not utter a word. He went into his closet, removed his clothes, and then headed straight to the bathroom. He showered for about twenty minutes.

Thoughts of him with another woman entered my mind, and I started to get enraged. I bet she was smaller than me. I bet when they had sex, he was able to lift her up and carry her to the bed, or have sex while holding her up with her legs wrapped around his mid-section. I always wanted my man to be able to pick me up and make love to me with my legs wrapped around him. I used to see those love scenes on television where the scene would start in the kitchen, and the man would lift the lady up and put her on the counter. Then, he would put her legs around him and carry her to the table then to the sofa then to the bedroom. Of course, the woman in the scene was probably a size two, which made it very easy for a man to pick her up. I had to laugh to myself when I thought of my husband trying to lift my big ass! Ron is not a big man at all, I would probably put him in the hospital with all this ass for him to have to carry.

When Ron finally finished his shower, he got into bed. Before he pulled the cover over him, I started in on him.

"Where'd you go? Over your bitch's house? I know the game, Ron. You took a shower before you left here. Then, you just take off and come back five hours later and take another shower. You think I'm stupid? Oh sure, I know you went out and got the woman you been wanting to be with all this time. What is she Ron, a size two?"

"What are you talking about? You have the nerve to try to turn this on me like you have no ownership or don't give a damn about what you did? Frankly, your excuse for oversleeping does not add up, and you're accusing me of fucking around. You sound like the guilty one, so don't bring that other woman shit up to me. I talked to Michael, and we both are confused about how both of you overslept. Something is not adding up, and I'm going to get to the bottom of it."

"Good way to avoid it, Ron. Who is she? Just tell me. I've been knowing all along that I'm not your type. All you had to do is just tell me. Yeah, you say you like women my size, but deep down inside I know it's all a lie."

"Why do you make everything about your size? Every time I get mad at you about anything, you turn it into me not being happy with you because of your size. I'm tired of hearing this shit about your weight. I told you over and over again that I'm very happy with you as you are. If you don't like the way you are and how you look, then do something about it and stop hounding me. I've had enough, and this bullshit has got to stop, Sam!"

"You just confirmed it for me, Ron. How you responded to me just now let's me know that there is someone else."

"Goddamn it, Sam! There's no fucking body else! Can you get that through your brain? I'm just tired of you beating yourself up about your weight, your size, or whether I'm attracted to you over a smaller woman. You need to get help. If only you could see the beauty I see when I look at you. The problem is that you have never seen the beauty in you, and that's sad."

We sat in silence for a couple of minutes and tears slowly trickled down my face. I was sitting on the edge of the bed, and Ron got up and came over to me. Then, he just held me while I cried. I cried so hard that I knew Ron was thinking that it was more to it. It *was* more to it. I was crying because of my size. I was crying because I wanted to be a size eight. I was crying because of trying crack cocaine to get to a smaller size. I was crying because I forgot about my children, and I was crying because I have a wonderful husband who loves me. However, I couldn't see that because I was so hung up over my size that nothing else mattered. I had to get that weight off of me.

After I finished crying, Ron and I made love for four hours. We started off just by caressing and kissing each other. We made sure that every body part was touched. After we caressed and kissed every body part, we played a game that we often played. Each of us got an opportunity   to entice the other. Whoever held out the longest without reaching an orgasm won. The winner got all of their favorite things done during the next act and didn't have to please their partner at all. It's kind of a selfish game, but both of us would get satisfied during the enticing part of the game. It just determined who could hold out the longest when someone was licking,   kissing,   and caressing the most sensitive areas. Ron always liked that game, because he says it made him be able to last longer during sex. I would have to agree, because there have been times when I wanted it to be over, but he was still going strong.

Ron won the game. I knew he was going to win, because he started at the top of my head and made his way down to Ms. Kitty. Once he found Ms. Kitty's sensitive spot, he caressed it gently with his tongue. Within one minute, it was over, and it felt so good. I had been so horny after smoking that crack. I just couldn't hold it. Ron was smiling because the next round would be all about pleasing him since he won. I knew exactly what he wanted, too. Rocky liked for me to put ice in my mouth while I massage my lips up and down on him.

While Ron was getting Rocky ready, I went downstairs to get a glass of ice and cup of hot water from the water cooler in the kitchen. When I arrived back upstairs, Ron and Rocky were waiting. Ron had Rocky in his hands gently massaging him. He knew I was going downstairs for the ice, but when he saw the other cup, he wanted to know what was in it. I told him it was hot water. He looked at me very suspiciously, and I didn't say a word. About a month or so ago, I was reading a story of a woman who drunk hot water right before orally entertaining her partner, it sent him wild. I wanted to try that on Ron to see if it had the same effect on him, especially if I rotated from the hot water to the cold ice.

I sipped at the hot water and stirred it around in my mouth so that my lips and tongue were nice and hot. Once I massaged my lips over Rocky, Ron went wild. He moaned, groaned, and screamed like I never heard him before. I continued to massage Rocky with my hot mouth until all the hot water was gone. Then, I removed an ice cube from the glass and sucked on it until my mouth had cooled off. Again, I continued my seduction with Rocky. At last, Ron exploded with pleasure. He screamed so loud that Ronda was knocking at the door saying she was scared because she heard some loud noises. I jumped up and reassured her that it was our television and sent her back to bed. Ron laid back in the bed in pure pleasure. I laid on his chest and we both drifted off to sleep.

CHAPTER 8

I t's been one month, and everything is back to normal with Ron and Michael. They are no longer angry with Lil and me. I know Ron has been very happy since we played that game. He requested the hot water and ice twice since then. I told Lil about it, and she tried it with Michael Sr. After they tried it, she told me that I should have told her about it months ago, because Michael Sr. had been bringing her flowers and calling her just to say he loved her. Once you figure out what a man loves, and then you give it to him, he's pretty much predictable from there. Lil and I have still been planning our next purchase of crack. We just can't stop thinking about it. We had to make sure all the bases are covered first. Also, I have not forgotten Ron's comment that he was going to get to the bottom of why Lil and I overslept. I'm hoping he forgot about it, but I need to be very careful.

Lil and I both applied for a credit card and received them last week. We purchased a post office box and used that as our address so that our husbands would not know anything about them. We will have the bills from the credit card going to that address. We needed the credit cards for booking a room at the hotel so we can smoke the crack. With Ron and Michael Sr. home, we couldn't do it in the house. Lil said Michael would be out of town next week. Ron would be leaving next month, and he would be gone for a week. We couldn't wait that long. Sam and Michael Jr. will start football practice tomorrow. Ronda and Michele will start cheerleading practice as well. Lil reserved a room for us at the Marriott Hotel located three miles from the school where the kids will be practicing. She requested a smoking room. The Marriott had a limited amount of "smoking" rooms. They explained that since smoking is not allowed in most places, the majority of their rooms are "non-smoking" and that the "smoking" rooms do not have the latest upgrades.

During lunch, we are going by Melvin's to pick up another eight ball. We told our husbands that we were going shopping after we dropped the kids off at practice. A few of the parents all take turns on staying with the kids during practice and dropping them off at home. We pulled up to Melvin's house and Lil went in to purchase the crack. She was in there for quite a while. I began to get worried. Once she came out of the house and got into the car, I let her have it.

"What the hell took you so long? Don't you know that we can get caught, and we have to get back to work!"

"Calm down. Everything is fine. We were just chillin. I guess he was just feeling me out to make sure everything was legit."

"What the hell does that mean, Lil?"

"He was flirting a little to see if I would take the bait."

"Well, did you? I've been out here long enough for you to take the bait!"

Lil rolled her eyes, but I noticed she had a weird look on her face.

"Lil! I know you did not mess around with Melvin!"

"No, I did not fuck Melvin, if that's what you're asking. Like I said, he was flirting trying to get me to go out with him."

We did not have enough time to get a quick hit before going back to work, so we stopped at McDonald's and got a quarter pounder meal and a diet coke. Regular coke has a lot of sugar so we figure we could save a couple of calories. Since we started this experiment, I have lost twelve pounds. Lil looks like she has lost much more than that. We were supposed to weigh in weekly, but it's funny how we don't think of weight anymore. All we think of is getting high, and we never mention our weight at all anymore. We got our food and went back to work.

After I got home from work, I fed my children some dinner, gathered all their gear in the car, and swung by to pick up Lil and her kids. We dropped the girls off first to their cheerleading practice. The coach would take them home around 9:00 p.m. Once we arrived at the football practice with the boys, Sam and Michael grabbed their equipment and headed towards the field. Another parent, Mrs.

Brown, would be dropping them off this week. It would be my turn the next week. Once the kids were settled, Lil and I headed straight to the hotel to get the high we had been craving for a month.

CHAPTER 9

When we arrived at the hotel, we parked in the back of the building and entered through the rear entrance. The "smoking" room was located on the ground floor also in the back of the building. Although it did not have the latest upgrades, it was nice and clean. We had stopped at the local convenience store to get sodas, cigarettes, lighters, and candles. Once we entered the room, I dampened a couple of the bath towels and placed them at the bottom of the door so the smoke would not escape from the room. I set the alarm clock for 8:00 p.m. so that we would make sure we were home when the kids got there. We were only about ten minutes away from our home. Nobody would suspect us to be at a hotel so close to home.

Therefore, it was the perfect plan. A repeat from a couple of months ago would not be good, and there would be no excuse that I could provide to Ron that he would accept.

Lil had the candles lit, and there were two cigarettes burning. We thought about using a pipe this time, but neither of us wanted to be seen buying it. So we decided to continue with the cheap way of using the cans and ashes. We smoked four of the eight packs of crack that we had just purchased from Melvin, and we were so high. The only problem was that the high did not last long. Once we took a hit and continued until the little rock disappeared from the ashes, the high would last no more than fifteen minutes before we were ready to open up the other pack and smoke more. This is a very expensive habit, and we can't afford to drop $200 every day to get high. I don't know what we are going to do, because the need is there and that is all I can think about. At this point, I just want to get high and enjoy this feeling. I feel like I'm on top of the world and that I can fuck all night. Damn, this crack makes me so horny.

After I snapped out of my daze, I looked over at Lil, and she was losing her mind. She kept scratching and smacking her arm because she thought something was crawling on her.

Then, she would jump up, run to the window, and peak out because she thought somebody was following her. I swear, watching her blows my high. Still, I have to try to contain my composure, because it affects her different from the way it affects me. I get horny and feel as though I'm invincible, and she gets paranoid, thinks everyone is after her, and that bugs are crawling on her. From my perspective, I think I have the better end of the deal, but high is high, and we should have never started on this journey anyway.

When the alarm clock started buzzing, Lil jumped up and ran out of the hotel room screaming. I jumped up and ran after her to try to calm her down. She was agitated and distraught. Guests started opening their room doors to see what all of the commotion was about. I explained to them that she had just got some very bad news and was very upset. I caught up to Lil after chasing her around the building two times. I was pissed! I wasn't in shape to be chasing her around this damn building. Plus, this crack already has my heart beating fast, and running after her did not help. I thought I was going to die. Finally, I calmed Lil down and got her to go back to the room to get our stuff so we could meet the kids at home. I'm glad I set the clock twenty minutes ahead of the actual time, or we would have been late. When we got into the car heading home, Lil was still freaked out but she was calming down. Her eyes looked as though they were bulging out from her face.

"Lil, you can't go home like this. You have got to get it together. Your kids will know something is up with you."

"What did you do with the four packs that were left?" she asked.

"I have them in my purse."

Damn, she didn't even respond about the kids. All she ever thinks about now is a rock.

"I want my half now. You can't take them all."

She was agitated and annoyed.

"Lil, I was not going to take them all. I was going to split with you, but since you thought someone was after you and all the ruckus you raised with the other guests coming out of their rooms, we needed to get out of there fast. We could not risk being seen."

"Give me mine now so you don't forget."

Wow, I couldn't believe her. She actually thought I was going to keep all of the crack for myself.

"Lil, please be careful and don't smoke this when the kids are around. They can't see you like this."

I gave Lil her two packs. She grabbed them… Actually, she snatched it from my hands and put them in her purse. She was off the hook. I should have kept them. Lord knows I wanted to, but I didn't want to fight with her. Plus, she fucked up my high thinking someone was after her when the alarm went off. When we arrived back at my house, the kids were not there. We had some time to go in and try to make ourselves look normal. I poured us a glass of Merlot from the bottle Ron and I shared last evening. I planned to serve the kids leftover spaghetti from last evening as well. I fixed Lil and me a plate of spaghetti. We sat down, ate the spaghetti, and drank the wine. Again, we did not talk much. This was so strange for us. We could never sit in a room together and not have anything to say.

We had both come down from our high, and all I could think of was taking another hit. I'm sure that is why Lil was quiet as well. We knew we could not risk it with the kids coming home in any minute. So, we just sat there and stared at each other. We must have sat there staring at each other for about twenty minutes, because we were both startled when we heard the door from the garage open. Ron had made it home.

"There's my two favorite ladies. You two look like you just got some bad news. What's up?"

"We are just worried about the kids. They should have been here by now."

"It's 8:45. I thought they were supposed to be here by 9:00?"

"Oh that's right. We're sitting here worrying ourselves silly," I said and forced a laugh.

Lil said, "Ron I told her not to worry and that the kids would be fine."

I cut my eyes at her as if to say, *you sellout*, but I laughed it off. I had to think of something to say to cover up how we were actually feeling. Minutes later, the kids were coming through the door. They were hungry, grumpy, and tired. I fixed all four of them a plate of spaghetti and a small salad. They barely said a word while they devoured their food as if they had not eaten in months. After they were done, Michael and Michele were ready to go home. Lil said her goodbyes to Sam and Ronda. After she bid farewell to them, she came in the kitchen where I was putting the dishes in the dishwasher and gave me a hug. During the hug, she whispered in my ear that she had to take a hit tonight. She asked me to wish her luck that she doesn't get caught. I held her firmly and whispered back in her ear and told her not to do it. She released her hold and summoned for the kids to go. I said a silent prayer for her and hoped that she would not slip and get us caught. I have too much to lose.

CHAPTER 10

I could not sleep at all because all I could think of was whether Lil was attempting to smoke the two bags of crack she had on her. I prayed that she did not try to do it in her home. Ron kept asking me if I was ok, and I told him that I was fine. So that he did not get suspicious after he kept asking me what was bothering me, I told him that I felt really bad about making him angry at me because I forgot to pick the kids up. He said that he was no longer mad. I thought to myself, *good, now he won't try to investigate further.* I was still a little horny from the crack I smoked earlier, so I put my arms around Ron and pulled his face close to mine. I softly stated to him that I was going to go take a shower and then I wanted to make it up to him when I returned. Then, I whispered that I just might have to boil some hot water. Ron just about lost his composure when he heard that.

Little did he know, I had more tricks up my sleeve than just the hot water and ice chips. That was getting old. Although Ron loved it, I craved more satisfaction. My desire to experiment seemed to significantly increase since I started smoking crack. It seemed that is all I wanted to do was smoke crack and fuck.

Some days, I wanted some good hard fucking. Other days, I wanted the sensuality and romance. The only challenge I had was that I had to experiment with Ron cautiously, so that he wouldn't think something was up or that I was having an affair.

Once I finished my shower, I went into my walk-in closet, which was located in the bathroom in an opposite corner from Ron's walk-in closet. I pulled out the Halloween outfit I purchased two years ago; it was a hooker costume. I did not have the nerve to wear it out that year when I purchased it, so it just sat in my closet all this time. I plan to get good use of it tonight. Ron was not in the bedroom when I exited the bathroom. Once I told him about the hot water, he was so excited that he couldn't contain himself. So he said he was going to make sure the kids were asleep were asleep. I slipped on the short mini skirt from the costume along with the black fishnet stockings and a red sequin halter top. To top off the outfit, I put on a pair of five-inch stilettos. I never wore those shoes out anywhere because I couldn't walk in them with all of the weight. The intent was only for the bedroom.

Ron had not showered yet, so I ran a bath for him in our Jacuzzi tub. I lit the candles surrounding the tub and turned off the lights in the bathroom. I had poured myself a glass of Cabernet Sauvignon that I pulled from the cellar. It was one of my favorites. When Ron and I visited Napa Valley a couple of years ago, I bought two cases of it. I poured Ron a glass of Prunier VSOP Grande Cognac from Champagne, France. This is one of his favorites. When Ron came back from ensuring that the kids were asleep, it was about eleven o'clock. They had a long day and would sleep through what I had planned.

Ron saw me in my hooker outfit and said "Goddamn, Baby! You look fine as hell!"

He commanded me to stand still so he could get a good look at me in my outfit. As he walked towards me, he looked around and saw the candles and bath waiting for him. Before he could say anything, I started undressing him. He started to help me, but I stopped him and whispered to him to let me do it. I told him that I was in control. He stopped trying to assist me and put his hands on my ass. I pushed them away and gave him the rules.

"Tonight, you are not allowed to touch. I am in control of providing you unsurmountable pleasure. All I need you to do is enjoy and let me do my work."

I handed my sexy husband his glass of cognac and guided him to the tub. Rocky was standing at full attention. I wanted Rocky so bad, but I had to maintain my coolness. If I was going to be in control, I needed to pace myself and enjoy every moment of the experience. Once Ron was seated in the tub with his drink in hand, I hit the remote control for the Bose sound system that had my iPod docked in it. I had it on the lovemaking playlist. The first song that played was "Freak Me" by Silk. The lyrics sang out, *"Let me lick you up and down 'til you say stop. Let me play with your body, baby, make you real hot. Let me do all the things you want me to do. 'Cause tonight, baby, I wanna get freaky with you."*

I begin to sing along with the song as I moved my body slowly to the music. Once I danced over to the tub where Ron was watching me intently, I kneeled down in my five-inch stilettos and gently washed his entire body, saving Rocky for last. I slowly removed my hooker outfit and stilettos and joined Ron in the tub. I gave him a sponge rinse over his entire body. When I got to Rocky, who was still standing at attention, I gently washed him with the bath sponge. After I was sure Rocky was nice and clean, I began to gently rub and massage him. Using one hand with my thumb and forefinger in the shape of a U, I gently stroked Rocky up and down for a few minutes. After that, I added circular motions. At that point, Ron was moaning so loud that I knew that I would have to let him release his pressure, and then go for round two.

Next, I alternated between one hand and two hands. I was able to stimulate both his shaft and the top of his penis. This drives Ron wild, and he always enjoys it when I switch between hands while giving him my famous hand massage. Rocky was ready to explode, so I did one final act to get him there. I went back to using one hand, and instead of the "U" shape, I made an "O" shape with my index finger and thumb and put it over Rocky. The "O" shape focused on the top of his penis which is the most sensitive. I slowly moved it up and down about an inch or so to stimulate the top. This is where the highest concentration of nerve endings is, which is why it is so sensitive. As I slowly massaged in circular motions, Ron was moving faster. I continued my circular movement and tried not to move too fast. He finally reached his peak and his liquid exploded all over my hands, arms, and the wall. While Ron recovered from the intense orgasm he had just experienced, he reached for me so that he could satisfy me orally. I stopped him and reminded him that I was in control and it was my night to please him.

I ran more water in the bath tub while Ron was still in it. I put a few drops of jasmine oil into the water and got back in it with my husband. Rocky was ready for round two. I had my back facing Ron, so I gently turned to him and asked if he was ready to go surfing. When he agreed, I guided Rocky into my warm tunnel and began to slowly grind in circular motions.

Ron joined in, and we both surfed together in a rhythmic motion that felt so amazing. We could barely hold our composure, and we had to try to keep the noise level down so the kids would not wake up. Ron was pumping so hard; and the harder he pumped, the more I wanted. Water was splashing everywhere. Since he had a release earlier, he was going much longer this time, and I wanted to reach my climax when he reached his. He pumped, and I rode him harder and harder until I lost it! We both screamed and held on to each other so tightly due to the intensity of the surf. Ron had scratches on his thighs from my grip. It was so intense. It was so beautiful. It was so damn good. That crack is something else.

CHAPTER 11

The alarm clock went off at 5:30 a.m. I really don't know how or when Ron and I made it to our king size bed after our intense sex in the bathtub. We were cuddled up in each other's arms and holding each other so tightly that we must have drifted off to sleep. I unleashed myself from Ron's embrace and rolled over to hit snooze on the alarm clock. What an amazing night... I still wanted more sex. For the life of me, I couldn't understand why I was so horny. I gently placed my hand on my vagina, and I was dripping wet. I feel like I was in heat or something. I looked at the clock and then looked back at Ron sleeping so peacefully. My vagina was throbbing for more of Rocky. I thought to myself, I *have to get rid of this desire within me*. I put my head under the cover and gently moved down to where Rocky was resting his limp body. Even in his limp state, he was about eight inches long. Once he was fully erect, I know he had to be about ten or eleven inches. I slowly placed him into my mouth and massaged up and down, ensuring that I used some of my saliva to make him moist. Rocky began to expand and that's when Ron woke up.

"Baby, what is going on with you? Damn, don't stop. That feels so good. Aww, damn baby."

Once Rocky was at his maximum length, I came up for air and straddled Ron. I easily guided Rocky into my warm vagina that was even wetter than before.

"Wow baby, you are so wet. You feel so good. I can't get enough of you," Ron moaned as he gripped my ass.

Once I had Rocky right where I wanted him, I begin to ride him like it was my last time. I don't know what got into me, but I had such an urge to fuck that I forgot where I was. I was like a wild woman. I rode that dick so hard that Ron could barely keep up. When I reached the final climax, I felt like fireworks went off in my head, and I lost consciousness for a few seconds. I laid on top of Ron for a minute to recover. When I sat up to look at him, he was staring at me in awe.

"What the fuck is going on with you, baby? You never ever gave it to me like that before. Are you fucking around on me?"

"No baby! I don't know what happened. You just turned me on so much last night, and when I woke up this morning, I was throbbing for more. You think I may be starting to go through the change? I hear that when a woman gets pre-menopausal, she gets very horny."

"I don't know, but if that's the case, I hope it is happening. Damn, I have never been fucked like that. You turned me out. The way you move that ass, um um um. Damn!"

Ron kept screaming, "Damn," and looking at me. He was so happy, and I must say that, I did turn him out. I finally got myself together and got up after the alarm went off the second time. It was 5:40 a.m., too damn early. I jumped in the shower, pulled out a black suit and a royal blue blouse that did not need ironing, put lotion on my body, got dressed, and went downstairs to wake the kids and fix their breakfast. Ron was still sitting on the bed watching my every move. He had a look of amazement on his face but also a look of concern. I think he was wondering where did all of that energy and endurance come from so suddenly. I smiled at him, kissed him passionately, and left the room. If only he knew that his wife was smoking crack, which made her horny as hell! Would he divorce me if he found out since I fucked him so well? *You just wait Ron, baby. There is a lot more where that came from, 'cause I could sure use a good hit right now.*

After I dropped the kids off at school, I arrived at work around 7:30 a.m. I tried calling Lil three times, and she didn't answer. I went down to her office, and she was not in yet. She usually gets in around 7:30 as well. This was not like her. I hoped she didn't do anything stupid after she left my house. Lil's boss, John, saw me as I was leaving her cubicle area. He knows that Lil and I are best friends.

"Hi Samantha. Where's Lily? She is usually here by now."

"I know. I guess she must be running late. If I talk to her, I will let her know that you were looking for her."

"Great, I just want to go over the milestone report with her."

"OK, John. I will let her know."

When I got back to my desk, I called Lil's cell phone repeatedly until she finally answered.

"Lil! Where are you? Your boss is looking for you to go over some Milestone report. Are you coming in? What's going on?"

I didn't give her an opportunity to answer any of my questions. I just went on and on.

"Did you do something crazy last night?

What happened? Did you get caught? Where are Michael Jr. and Michele? Where is Michael Sr.? Are you at home?"

Lil screamed in my ear.

"Sam! Get a grip! Can I please get a word in?"

I stopped my ranting and listened to what Lil had to say. "Someone is following me. I'm pulled over in the parking lot at Walmart so that they can pass me. I was on the way in and this guy in a black 300M kept looking at me. I think he is after me, Sam! I took the next exit to escape him. He didn't follow me, but I have been sitting here for an hour to make sure the coast is clear."

Lil is losing her fucking mind. I had to be very careful on how I responded to her.

"Maybe he was looking at you because you are pretty Lil. I'm sure that's all it was. You know you always have the guys going crazy with that long beautiful hair, caramel-colored skin, and that badonkadonk you got trailing behind you. Why do you think he was following you?"

"I just know he was!" Lil was hysterical. "OK. Do you think you can make it in, or do you need me to come get you?"

"I think I am going to try to make it in." "OK, good. Call your boss and tell him you had car trouble and that you are on your way."

"OK, I will call him now, and then I should be in the office in twenty minutes." "Great. Call me when you get in." "OK. I will."

I didn't want to ask Lil if she smoked the two bags of crack last night. By the way she was acting with the paranoia, I'm almost certain she did. I just don't know how she pulled it off. I had to find out what she did. I was itching to finish my two bags as well, and I wanted Lil and me to take a long lunch today so I could calm the urge. However, I couldn't risk anyone finding out what I was doing. I had to maintain control over the crack. It was getting harder, because the urge to smoke was always there in the forefront of my mind and my thoughts.

Lil called me when she arrived at work and said that she was going in to meet with her boss. She told me that she had a sneaky suspicion that her boss was the one who had the guy in the black 300M follow her. She said she was going to go into his office and act like she didn't know, but she was going to keep a close eye on him. I told her that we needed to get out of the office for lunch. She said should could not go until one o'clock. I agreed, but waiting that long was going to drive me insane. *How could I maintain the constant feigning like I'm just fine, while inside, my body is craving another hit?* Lil was not ready to go to lunch until 1:30. When she called, she informed me that she told her boss that she was leaving for the remainder of the day. That meant that I had to figure out how I was also going to get off for the rest of the day. As an Executive Assistant, it is hard to just take off on the whim when your boss relies on you for his schedule and running the office.

Just as I was sitting at my desk trying to think of an excuse, my boss buzzed for me to come into his office. Once I entered, he asked me to clear his calendar for the remainder of the day, and then he told me that he was leaving early to take care of some business. I told him that I would call and inform his clients and see what time was best for them next week. Before I left his office, I asked him if he had any concerns with me leaving after I cleared his calendar. He said that he was going to tell me to take off for the remainder of the day anyway because the week would be a light week. However, the following week, he would need me to be on board and ready to put in extra hours. I cancelled Daniel's appointments for the rest of the day. I had to reschedule them for the week after next because his schedule was completely booked for the following week. Visitors from Silicon Valley were going to be in town and there were meetings scheduled with all of the departments to discuss reorganizational changes.

I finally arrived at Lil's office at 1:45. I told her that I was able to get the remainder of the day off. She wanted to go to her house, but she said that she had a stop to make first. When I gave her an inquisitive look, she gave me a look back that said, "don't mess with me." I didn't pry. I simply said ok and that I would come over when she got back. She gave me that same evil-look again and told me that she needed me to go with her. I agreed and did not ask any questions, because deep down inside, I knew exactly where we were headed. However, she didn't ask for any money, so that had me extremely concerned. She said that Michael Sr. had a client in town and would be home late, so she wanted to avoid paying for a hotel. She also said that since we have only done it at my house, we should switch up so the smell does not get into the carpet and curtains. That reminded me that I needed to wash the curtains and steam clean the carpet in the guest room where Lil and I took our first hit of crack. When I went in there the other night, there was a faint smell of smoke.

Lil insisted that she drive. I felt a little awkward about her driving, since she always seemed to think someone was after her.

However, if I forced the issue and said that I would drive, she would create a scene. Her behavior had been unpredictable lately, and any minor thing would set her off. I told her that I would follow her to her house to park my car, and then we could leave for her stop. So, we dropped my car off and headed to wherever Lil needed to go. Just as I suspected, she pulled up at Melvin's house. She told me that I did not have to be inconspicuous anymore, because he knew that the crack was for her.

"What! You told him that you are smoking crack, Lil?"

"I didn't tell him, Sam. He figured it out.

He said that he has been selling drugs for a long while and can spot when someone is on them.

"Damn, Lil! Does he know that I do it as well?"

"No… I told him that you have been trying to help me so that Michael Sr. won't find out." "Yea, sure. And I'm sure he believes that just as much as me saying I'm a size two! "We are fucked!"

"Don't worry. We are going to be fine." Lil jumped out of the car and ran up to

Melvin's door. He seemed to open it immediately, which told me that he was probably watching us. I kept my head down so that if Melvin or someone else was looking out the window, they would not get a good view of my face. I looked in the back seat to see if Lil had a newspaper back there so that I could cover my face more. She didn't have a newspaper, but she did have a scarf. I pulled the scarf from the back seat and wrapped it around my neck. Then, I took the part of the scarf that was hanging down and placed it up to my mouth so that part of my face was covered. I know I looked foolish because it was eighty-two degrees on a beautiful June day, and I had a scarf wrapped around my face like it was a thirty-two-degree day in December.

I waited in the car for Lil for an hour.

What the hell was she doing in there? I was so mad. I wanted to go and ring the doorbell, but just as I was getting the nerve up to go to the door, Lil came out. She was high already! When she got in the car, she would not make eye contact with me. That was a dead giveaway of her guilt.

"You fucked him didn't you? Is that why you didn't ask me for any money to go in half with you? What did you do for it, Lil?"
"Look Sam, I refuse to keep spending money on a hotel and an eight ball every other day. Michael Sr. is going to find out if we continue at that pace. You're right. I did fuck him. I had a quickie with Melvin so that he would give me what I wanted. You always said he had a crush on me anyway, and you were right… He does. He's a bad lay, but I got another eight!"

I didn't say another word to Lil the entire drive back to her house. I was so mad at her.

How could she do that to Michael? I hope she used protection. There are too many diseases out here to take chances like that. When we arrived back at Lil's house, Michael was still at work and the kids were still at school. They had practice after school, so we had quite a bit of time to ourselves to smoke. We went downstairs in the basement in one of the guest rooms. I could tell Lil had smoked in there before because there was a halfway burned candle and a candle lighter in the room. The room had a fresh mountain breeze smell to it. It was coming from the plugged-in air freshener that was in the electrical outlet by the door. I pulled out my phone and set the alarm for 6:30 p.m. That would give us time to get to the school to get the kids from practice at seven o'clock. I was so mad at Lil on the ride back from Melvin's house that I forgot to tell her to stop so we could get some soda and use the cans like we always did to smoke our crack.

"Shoot! Lil, we forgot to stop and get the sodas."

"We don't need to use soda cans anymore. Melvin gave me a glass pipe. He also showed me how to make my own pipe using a lightbulb."

"A lightbulb? Aren't we fancy? And, just when did Melvin show you all of this? Seems like you have been frequenting Melvin more often than you are saying? What's up with that?"

"I only went to visit him twice without you knowing about it."

"And, what happened while you were there long enough for him to show you how to make your own pipe and for him to give you your own pipe?"

"Nothing happened, Sam!"

"You're lying through your fucking teeth, Lil. You know you can't lie to me. You fucking him for rocks?"

"It's not like that Sam. I will tell you all about it. Just please let me take my hit first. I promise I will tell you. I need to get this off my chest anyway."

***

Lil had already had a pack of lightbulbs in the nightstand drawer in the room where we were smoking. She already had a homemade pipe made from a lightbulb, but she gave me the pack of light bulbs so that I would take one out and learn how to make my own. I took a standard lightbulb from the box. Lil told me to take the lightbulb and cover the glass part with the towel she handed me. I was instructed to leave only the metal part that you would screw into a socket exposed. She gave me the scissors that she also had stored in the nightstand drawer. Then, she told me to snip off the metal tip on the end by gently pinching the bottom of the metal rim to squeeze the black part under the metal tip until it cracked.

The black part broke into tiny pieces with some of the pieces flying onto the carpet. I pulled the remaining pieces off, and I could now look inside of the lightbulb. There was a glass tube inside with some other type of stuff. Lil told me to take the scissors and put it inside the open hole on the lightbulb and break the glass. That did not take any effort at all to do. As soon as I stuck the scissors into the hole and moved it back and forth, it broke. I turned the bulb upside down to get the broken glass out, but it would not come out. As I looked over at Lil for additional instructions, she was pacing back and forth in her usual paranoid manic way. I was annoyed because she was high as hell and there I was trying to make a homemade pipe, and I still hadn't taken a hit yet. I was feeling like that was intentional. As a result, I jumped up and grabbed the glass pipe that Melvin gave to Lil, put some rock on it, and took a hit. Man! That hit felt so good. I had to sit down and enjoy the high. After about five minutes, I took another hit. I was feeling the effects of the crack on me, and I could not sit still. I turned my focus back to the homemade pipe that was in the making.

Lil was still pacing back and forth, and I had to get her to focus.

"Lil, the glass won't come out. What do I do next?"

Lil went to the door of the room, peeked out, and closed it.

"Lil! What do I do next?"

She came over and looked at the lightbulb that I was working on and told me that I needed to cut out the filament. I used the scissors to snip it. Then, I turned the lightbulb upside down, and the glass and filament fell out on the towel. Some white powder came out as well. Lil told me that it would dissolve when I took my first hit. If I rinsed it out, I would not be able to use it right away because it would take a while to dry. I took her word for it because I did not want to wait. I wanted to use my own pipe and not share with Lil, so I left the powdery residue inside the lightbulb and hoped that it didn't cause me any harm when I inhaled my first hit. I looked at the lightbulb and knew something was missing. I just had a lightbulb with the insides removed and the black tip at the bottom of the metal part removed. *How in the world is this a homemade pipe?* This time Lil saw me looking at the pipe and laughed.

"You are not done yet, girl! You have one more step to go, and then you will be ready."

Lil unscrewed the top off of a water bottle that she had sitting on the nightstand and handed it to me. I looked at her like she was nuts. She told me to screw it onto the metal grooves on the lightbulb. Since I only removed the black metal tip from the bottom of the metal grooved part, the top to the water bottle twisted onto the lightbulb with ease. Lil then instructed me to use the scissors to make two holes in the water bottle top. At this point, she was strictly focused on what I was doing. She told me to make sure I didn't make the holes too big, because two straws were going to go in the holes. That's when she realized that she didn't have the straws in the room with us.

Immediately, she peeped out the door again, closed it, peeped out again, and ran out the room and up the stairs to get the straws from the kitchen.

When she got back less than two minutes later, she had a handful of straws. She gave me two of them and put the others in the nightstand drawer. She told me to cut one straw about four inches long and the other straw about six inches long. After that, I placed them in each hole on the bottle top, and I was ready to smoke my crack. I unscrewed the water bottle top from the lightbulb, and then I took a piece of the eight- ball that Lil was smoking from and put it into the bottom of the homemade pipe. I screwed the water bottle top back onto the lightbulb with the straws in place. The four-inch straw was pushed down so that only about one-half of an inch was sticking up from the hole. The six-inch straw was the straw I would use to inhale. All but about one inch of the inhalation straw was protruding out of the lightbulb.

I grabbed the candle lighter and heated the bottom of the lightbulb where the rock was sitting until it produced smoke. I moved the candle lighter in circular motion so that the rock wouldn't burn. Once smoke started to form, I put my mouth on the six-inch straw and inhaled. Wow! This was a much better high than smoking the crack from the soda can. It was more potent. I feel like a lot of the product was being lost in the can due to the residue that built up in the inside of the can. The residue was probably the best part of the drug. Little did I know that I could have collected the residue and smoked that, because it was in its purest form when it burned down and the residue collected inside the can. I found that out from Lil. She suddenly seemed to know a lot about how to smoke. I think she had been sneaking out and doing more crack by herself. I was pissed about it because she excluded me, and I also think she was tricking to get the crack.

I refused to continue to worry myself about any of that at the moment, because I didn't want to blow such an amazing high. If only I could stay in that state for the next two hours. Unfortunately, the high would last no longer than fifteen minutes before I'd have to take another hit. I took four additional hits before the alarm went off on my phone. It was time to head to the school and pick the kids up from practice. Lil was still pacing around the room and opening and closing the door. She would run out into the hall and run back in and close the door. She would then peek out the window, sit down for a minute or so, and repeat the same thing over and over and over again.

She could definitely blow your high if you paid attention to her being so paranoid.

I let her know that we had two rocks left, and we should finish them because we needed to go pick up the kids. She asked if I would pick them up while she stayed there and cleaned up all of the paraphernalia. I knew Lil was up to something, so I told her no; I was firm with my answer. It took her by surprise, because my voice was deep, firm, and matter of fact. She rolled her eyes, but she did not say a word. She simply picked up one of the rocks from the two that were left, placed it into her new glass pipe, and inhaled. I followed suit, because I was not going to let her have the last one. Minutes later, Lil began her paranoia routine while I enjoyed my last buzz.

Finally, it was time to go. We are supposed to be there to pick up the kids at seven o'clock, and it was ten minutes until that time. There was no way we would make it on time. When I grabbed my purse, took my keys out, and told Lil that it was time to go, she grabbed her purse and headed towards the door. She was pissed with me, but she needed to go with me because I didn't trust her ass. During the drive, I reminded Lil that she never got around to telling me about what was going on with her and Melvin. She quietly sighed and was silent for about five minutes. As I pulled up to the school to pick up the kids, Lil placed her hand on mine and said that she promised to tell me everything tomorrow.

CHAPTER 12

After we picked the kids up from practice, I dropped Lil and her crew off at home. Thank God Lil had calmed down enough that her kids did not notice much of a difference in her behavior. They just thought she was tired.

Michael was just getting home when I pulled into Lil's driveway. He came over to the car and greeted us. Michael Jr. and Michele jumped out of the car and ran to embrace their daddy. They loved him so much. I bid farewell to them after watching the brief reunion of the family. Michael and Lil embraced each other with such passion. It was a pleasure to see love like that. As I watched them, I could not help but wonder about what else Lil was up to with Melvin and what else she got herself into. It was bad enough that she slept with him.

When my kids and I arrived home, Ron was already there. He was in the family room watching TV. Ronda and Sam greeted their dad with the same passion that Lil's kids showed their father. Ronda ran to the family room and gave her daddy the biggest hug. Sam was too cool. He slowly walked to the family room and dapped up his dad. Although he did not show it, you could tell that he was happy to see Ron because of the big grin on his face. They acted as though Ron had been away for a month. Ron is not scheduled to travel extensively until next month. However, because he travels so frequently, Sam and Ronda always felt as though it was a treat to have him home.

While the kids hung out with Ron, I went into the kitchen to warm up the leftovers from last night. The phone rung while I was heating up the baked chicken and broccoli and cheese casserole. It was my sister Debra. This was unusual since it wasn't Sunday. Debra usually calls me every Sunday, but I hadn't talked to her since Lil and I started on our experiment.

"Hello," I answered.

"Well you do exist?" Debra had a bit of sarcasm in her voice.

"Yes I do. How are you, sis?"

"I'm good. I have been worried about you. We missed four Sundays talking. Why didn't you call me back?"

"I'm so sorry. I have been so busy with the kids with their practice, and my job is requiring me to work extra hours. It's just been crazy."

"Oh I'm sorry. I know you must be exhausted."

Ron entered the kitchen when I was telling Debra how exhausted I was because of working extra hours at work and the kids' practices. He gave me a weird and quizzical look. I knew I would hear about it later. Debra gave me an update on Marie's children. She had become a different person since she started raising Jason and Deidre. She seemed to be so happy. She wanted to bring them over for a visit and wanted to know what day would be good. I told her that I would check the schedule and get back with her. She then proceeded to tell me that Marie was still struggling, and she still had moments when she would disappear.

I thought to myself, she should know better and she gets what she deserves. Then, suddenly I felt a rush of anxiety and panic overcome my body. I began gasping for air and my heart was pounding so hard that I thought I was having a heart attack. I sat down in the chair at the kitchen table to catch my breath.

Ron noticed my sudden need for air and asked if I was ok. I told him that I was fine and that I just needed to catch my breath. He told me to take slow, deep breaths. He coached me through my breathing, and after about five minutes, I was back to breathing normally again. Ron said I had just had a panic attack and asked what prompted it. I told him that I didn't know, but that I felt an overwhelming sense of sadness after talking to Debra. He told me to not get myself so worked up about Marie and the kids that Debra was raising. I promised him that I would not.

Little did he know that the panic attack actually stemmed from me saying to myself that Marie knew better and that she gets what she deserves, when I am actually doing the same thing. How could I judge her and I was in the same boat. The only difference was that no one knew I smoked crack, and I was not strung out on it selling my body. I did it to lose weight, and I was down twenty-five pounds. However, I did not think I would get addicted to it. At least I was controlling my habit. Although I had the panic attack, I knew that I shouldn't have judged my sister. Nevertheless, I did feel that I was in control. I would never let myself go like Marie did. She lost her children for God's sake!

The next day, Lil and I took our lunch breaks together. We only had thirty minutes because Lil was on restriction for ninety days due to her late arrivals to work. Her manager told her that she could no longer take hour-long lunch breaks, because she was arriving to work late and then taking an hour and a half for lunch. To save time, Lil and I went to the McDonald's down the street and sat in the parking lot and ate our food. While we were eating, I asked Lil to update me on what is going on with her and Melvin, and she gave me an ear full. I was not prepared for the things she told me.

She started the conversation by telling me that she and Melvin had been having sex for the last two months. She thought he suffered from premature ejaculation, because it was so quick. She said she did it because she got her crack free in return. She went on to say that because she has been getting it free, that was all that she wanted. She couldn't think about anything else. She admitted that she hadn't been present for the kids like she usually was. Because Michael had been traveling so much, she had more time to do it at home. She said one night she left the house and went to Melvin's at 2:00 a.m. She left the kids at home sleep, and Michael was out of town. She said that she did not get back home until six o'clock the next morning, just in time to wake the kids up for school. I asked Lil what was she doing at Melvin's for four hours if he was a quick lay, and she said that he made her ride with him to one of the numerous crack houses he owns. I lost it when I heard that!

"What the hell do you mean he made you go to one of his crack houses? You mean to tell me that other people saw your face? How could you let that happen, Lil? What the fuck were you thinking? He has got you exactly where he wants you now! Look at you! You have lost so much weight that your face is starting to look to thin.

What if Michael finds out?"

"Sam, please chill out! I have everything under control. I was safe at the crack house - Melvin made sure of it. He kept a watch on me and kept me safe next to him. I was so zoned out, and Melvin made sure I didn't run out. He looks out for me, Sam. He really protects me, and all I have to do is lay there and count to five and he's done. I don't have to make no effort at all, and he is all in love and shit. He's such a bad lay, but I get what I want in the end."

"Lil, girl you are playing with fire. You can't be this naïve. You don't get what you need. Can't you see that? Girl, he owns you now. He can blackmail you and tell your husband! How stupid can you be? Please stop what you are doing. We can get it our old way. You don't need to have sex with him, if that is what you call it. What about your family? What about Michael?"

"My family has nothing to do with this.

They will never know anything about this," she snapped.

"How can you say that, Lil? As long as you are giving Melvin what he wants, your family is ok. What happens if you try to end it? What happens if you stop getting crack from him? I don't think it's going to be that easy to get away from him as you think it is? I swear, you better not get me involved in this shit."

"You are not and never will be involved.

Hold your horses, I got this…"

Lil went on to explain that since Melvin owns the house, he set the rules. She said that he has deals with pimps and prostitutes. He sets the prices and assigns the rooms for them to use, and he gets a cut. The male customers usually made deals for the prostitutes, and that is when they disappeared into one of the assigned rooms. The others are smoking crack or trying to sell items to Melvin and other drug dealers so they could get more drugs. She said that the place was not what you would think a normal crack house would look like. Because Melvin owns it, he has a crackhead cleaning it for him. If she doesn't do a good job, he cuts her off. Suddenly, I felt another rush of panic, but I started to breath in and out until my heart beats began to slow back to normal pace. Somehow, I knew deep down inside that I would regret Lil's last statement about me never being involved.

Lord help us all.

CHAPTER 13

School would be out for the summer break in two weeks. Ronda, Sam, Michael Jr., and Michele were going to stay with my parents for the entire summer. My parents insisted every year that Ronda and Sam spend the summer with them. About two years ago, Ronda and Sam complained so much about wanting Michael Jr. and Michele to go with them to South Carolina that my parents finally gave in. Since then, they have insisted that Michael Jr. and Michele come each time. They said they help keep each other entertained, which meant that all they had to do was feed them and take them here and there occasionally. They planned to take the kids to Disney World this time. They all are so excited.

Both couples, including me and Ron, usually send my parents a monthly allowance for the kids' activities and extra for them keeping the kids. They say we don't have to send it, but deep down, we all know that it does help.

Lil and I spent Saturday taking the kids shopping for their trip to South Carolina. We bought them clothes, shoes, pajamas, and necessities. After we finished shopping, we went to our favorite pizza place and had pizza and salad. It was late when we finished so, we headed home. During our day out with the kids, Lil was on edge. She was very impatient and seemed to be in a hurry. I knew what was on her mind; however, we could not let the kids see any difference in our mannerism. I gave Lil an evil eye, and she composed herself enough to get through the rest of the evening. When we got to my car to go home, Michael Jr. and Michele asked if they could stay the night with Ronda and Sam. I wanted to say no, but that would definitely be out of character. I told Michael Jr. and Michele that they could stay the night.

However, I knew it was a bad decision, because I was worried about what Lil was going to get herself into.

When Lil said she was going to go home to drop off their bags and get them some fresh clothes, I walked her out to her car and told her that I knew she was up to something. She said that Michael was home and that she was going to stay home. She gave me two rocks for me to smoke and said she would get more from Melvin tomorrow. I gladly took them. I planned to smoke them once I put the kids to bed. The problem was that I needed to look out for Ron. If he did not feel my warmth next to him in bed, he would come looking for me. I decided that I would tell him that I have work to complete for my job and that I would go into the basement to work on it. I hoped that tactic worked because I want to take a hit so bad and could not, and I was so enraged. My lovemaking to Ron was very unadventurous, but I ensured that he was very well pleased.

Lil had planned to retrieve the kids after church service the next morning. I got up to wake everyone up to get ready for church. To my surprise, Ron was already up and showering. I usually would have to wake him up at least three times. This is when I planned my scheme to get back home to smoke my crack. When Ron came out of the shower and into the bedroom, I was sitting at the edge of the bed holding my stomach. He came over to me and asked what was wrong. I told him that I was having severe cramps in my stomach and that it must have been the pizza I ate. I laid back on the bed and balled myself in a fetal position. Ron instructed me to stay home in bed, and he and the kids would go on to church. *Just what I wanted,* I thought to myself.

Once Ron and the kids left, I went into the guest room and put my two rocks on the night stand. I forgot that the pipe I made at Lil's a few weeks ago was in hidden in my trunk. I ran to the garage and retrieved my pipe, grabbed the phone, and locked myself in the guest room.

Thankfully, the guest room sits right over the garage, so I would hear Ron and the kids when they arrived home. I had my air freshener as well. I placed a piece of rock on the pipe and lit it. I felt so amazing. It felt good to smoke my crack without Lil. I was at peace because there were no doors slamming, I didn't have to watch Lil walk back and forth a million times.

**

The two weeks before summer break went by really fast! Lil and I were in the car headed to South Carolina to drop the kids off with my parents. We were staying for the weekend and then returning back home. We were more excited than the kids. We would be without kids and husbands for a whole two months! Michael and Ron partnered on a deal, and they would be out of the country visiting India, Japan, and Africa. Ron had been kinda tight-lipped about this deal. He said that it is huge and he did not want to jinx it by talking about it. He also said that if it went through, it would change our life tremendously.

It was three o'clock in the afternoon when we arrived at my parents' home. The drive was actually peaceful because the kids had their iPads connected through the hotspots that we have as part of the cell phone package plan.

They stayed connected on social media, watched videos, updated their statuses on Instagram, and sent short video clips on Vine of them in the car. Although I did all of the driving, Lil and I had great conversations. However, we talked in code majority of the ride down to my parents' house.

Mom had dinner ready when we got there.

We could smell the good ole southern cooking when we walked through the door. The aromas from collard greens, fried chicken, and cornbread filled the air. My mouth began to water and yearn for my mamma's southern cuisine. I could cook, but my cooking does not compare to my mamma's. We took the luggage to the guest rooms upstairs, washed our hands and faces, and came down for dinner. It was great to be home. My parents looked as though they had not aged in years. I am blessed to have such healthy parents. They actually had more energy than I did at times. Mom always scolded me by saying that I needed to learn to have more patience. She said that getting annoyed by the little things will make you age and have health problems. That didn't make sense to me when she said it to me back then, and it still does not make sense now. However, I'm starting to think she may have been on to something.

The next morning, after we went to church with my parents, Lil and I said our goodbyes and headed home. Ron and Michael phoned early in the morning letting us know that they made it to India safely. Because of the time zones, we would not be talking to them often. Ron said to send him text messages and he would see them when he woke up. Lil and I were so excited. We had no kids and husbands. We could do our crack in our own houses without sneaking. We both had taken two weeks off from work. Lil had a hard time getting her leave approved due to her probation, but they eventually granted it to her. I had to train one of the other admins on what I did before I left for vacation. It was no issue because she and I both had covered for each other before.

When we arrived back home, Lil and I dropped our bags in my family room and went upstairs to the guest room where I smoked crack in a few weeks ago. I had smoked all of my crack, but Lil said she had some on her. She pulled out her pipe, and I retrieved mine from the bottom drawer of the nightstand where it was hidden underneath some sheets. We smoked the crack for what seemed like days, but it was only about five hours. Lil had about eight rocks on her. We started smoking about four o'clock in the afternoon. By nine o'clock that night, we were both feening for more crack. I had never been that high before. My heart was pounding, and I felt like I was floating above the earth. I just wanted to stay in that state forever. I had no worries or cares, and it felt so amazing.

Crack still affected Lil the same way. Since no one was in my house, she was running out of the room and opening and closing all of the doors on the upstairs level where we were located. She thought someone was following her, so every thirty minutes, she went down to check the front door to ensure that it was locked.

Other than her paranoia episodes, it had been a pretty nice evening. We talked about everything - that is, once she sat down for a moment and stopped slamming the doors. Our conversations were so in depth. We even talked about what would happen if we were caught.

She began to spill more information on what she and Melvin had been doing. She gave me the inside scoop on how he runs his crack house. She said that she went with him twice to two other crack houses and they were really disgusting. Dirty condoms were strewn around, women were having sex right in front of everyone for a rock, the place smelled of urine, and they were in a very bad neighborhood. She went there with Melvin to pick up his money from the other drug dealers he does business with sometimes. I couldn't believe what she was telling me. I wanted more crack, but I have too much pride to put myself in that type of atmosphere.

After about another hour, Lil jumped up and said that she needed to go see Melvin. I told her that I would drive. Truth be told, I was glad she wanted to go see him, because I needed more crack and didn't want to say it. I know it's double standards - I don't want Lil to see Melvin because of her family, but it was okay when I wanted to get high. I was not a good friend for that, but when the monkey gets on your back, you have to get it off. Still, I hated what was happening to me with the crack. I seemed to lose my sense of morals, but I was glad that we were headed to get more. When we arrived at Melvin's, Lil went in and came out about five minutes later. I thought that was really quick and Melvin was much worse at sex than I had imagined.

Meanwhile, Lil got back into the car and slammed the door.

"That motherfucker won't even give me no more! He said I had enough and that I am smoking too much. He said he don't want his woman being no crack head, and he needs me to chill out."

"What? He's been giving it to you to get you hooked, and now he is trying to make you stop, Lil? That is not his decision!"

"It sure the hell isn't. I will fix his ass!

Drive. I know exactly where we are going."

I drove for about twenty minutes on Interstate 295 before we took an exit where we went through a tunnel. Next, Lil was telling me to park in front of some row houses. The neighborhood looked a little scary. There were folks out loitering and trash strewn around.

Some of the houses looked unkempt and ignored. Lil told me to get out and follow her. I had my reservations, but I wanted to get high so bad that I was not thinking logically. I thought that she knew someone here at this row house and that we could buy an eight ball from them. When we got to the front door of the row house, the door opened before Lil could even knock on it. A big burly guy stood there looking directly at Lil. When he finally opened his mouth, he asked her where was Melvin. Lil told him that Melvin was tied up and that he wanted her to pick up an eight from Que. The big burly guy gave Lil an inquisitive look, but he opened the door all the way and let both of us inside.

When we entered the house, I immediately smelled an awful stench. It smelled of urine and feces. I had to throw up but I held it. We were guided to the room to the right of the front door. I'm assuming it would be the living room in a normal home like this. When we entered the room, there was a woman on her knees giving a man a blow job. No one seemed to pay them any attention. The man looked like he could have been possibly a drug dealer. He had on nice clothing and jewelry from what I could tell. I started to panic. I hoped they did not expect me to perform any sex acts. My heart began to beat so fast, and I immediately begin to take deep breaths in and out. That was when Que walked in and Lil noticed my breathing. Que looked at me and asked Lil if I was okay. She explained that I am her close friend and that I had never been to a crack house before. I screamed when I heard that.

"A crack house! Lil, you brought me to a crack house!?"

"I am sorry!" she pleaded.

Just as I was getting ready to let Lil have it, Que interrupted and asked her if Melvin knew she was here. She gave him the same story that she gave to the big burly guy stating that Melvin asked her to get an eight from him. Que laughed. His laugh was deep and his whole body shook. He abruptly stopped in the midst of his laughter and forcefully grabbed Lil by the arm.

He put his face close to hers and told her that she had some fucking nerve. He threatened her to come clean, or he was going to call Melvin. To show Lil how serious he was, he pulled his cell phone from his right front pocket and instructed it to call Melvin. That is when Lil gave in and told him that she went to Melvin to get an eight, but he did not give it to her. She continued her story informing Que that she was there to buy an eight. Que hung up the phone. He asked Lil if she had any money. She said she had $200. Lil handed him the money, and he gave her the rocks. We began to head toward the door when the big burly guy stopped us.

"You are not going nowhere. Melvin told me to hold you two here. He is pissed that you tried to pull one over on him, so he is going to teach you a lesson. We have to hold you here until he arrives, and he says he won't be here until Monday."

The big burly guy licked his lips as he was making that statement and looked at me as though he had major plans for me. I looked at Lil in terror. She began to cry and scream and told them that they could not hold her hostage. She picked up her phone to call the police, and Que snatched it from her hand. She starting swinging and screaming, and Que grabbed her and put her in one of the rooms that was located off of the "living room" where the woman was giving the man a blow job. She never stopped bobbing her head up and down on his fully erect penis while all of this activity with Lil, myself, Que, and the big burly guy was going on.

Once Lil was in the room, I didn't hear anymore sounds from her. Que came out of the room as I continued standing there in horror. He looked at me and asked me what was my part in this scheme. I told him that I didn't know where we were going and that I am the driver. I told him I had no idea that the house was a crack house. He laughed again. It was the same laugh that he did earlier. Just as before, he cut it short, came face to face with me as well, and told me that he was no fool. He grabbed me by my arm, and the more I resisted, the harder his grip got. I finally gave in, and he dragged me to the same room where Lil was.

When I entered the room, Lil was sitting on an old beat up couch smoking one of the rocks she purchased. She was using her personal pipe that Melvin gave her. She had it in her purse. She began to apologize and cry. She told me that Melvin would probably really leave us there until Monday. She said she was done with Melvin. She could not believe that he would treat her that way. All I could think about was the stench I was smelling and the uncleanliness of the house. Lil handed me her pipe and told me to take a hit so that I could calm down. She instructed me to sit down. I looked at her as if she had lost her mind. I told her there was no way I was going to sit on the couch. She then told me to look at the floor. I slowly looked around and the floor was filled with debris that consisted of empty bottles, needles, and condoms. As I analyzed my situation, it turned out that the couch was the best option out of the two.

Although it was June, it was a little chilly when we left my house earlier, so I put on my light jacket that I keep in my car. I removed the jacket, laid it on the couch, and sat on it. At least my body would not come in contact with the couch, my jacket would serve as a buffer. I took one hit from Lil's pipe and then another. I immediately began to feel a calm come over my body. This is probably the only time when I would say that smoking crack was good for me. We had smoked about eight of the rocks from the twelve that Lil purchased from Que when we heard the door knob turn, and then Melvin entered the room. I had no idea what time it was. Que had also taken my phone from me.

Melvin walked in the room, looked me up and down, and went to Lil. He lifted her up off the couch and slapped her. Lil screamed. I gasped. I could not restrain myself, so I yelled at him.

"Hey, don't you hit my friend like that!

What kind of a man hits a woman?"

Melvin looked at me and threw Lil back down on the couch. Then, he came over to me. He grabbed me up and talked to me with a sly look on his face.

"Oh, you must be the driver. Lil said you didn't smoke it, but I knew she was lying. You are a crack head just like she is. I tried to protect her, but she went against my rules. If she plays by the rules, everything will be ok for her and you. You got that?"

I shook my head and looked over at Lil. He threw me on the couch and went back to Lil. He kissed her passionately and said he was sorry.

He told her that he loved her and wanted to help her. He told her to never disobey his rule again. Lil agreed and Melvin said he wanted to get us out of that hell hole. As we were leaving the house, the big burly guy gave us back our cell phones. It was over twelve hours later. We had been in that house since Sunday night around 11:00 p.m. until Monday at noon. The big burly guy was right. He said Melvin would not show up until Monday. Thank God I had no missed calls, but I did have two text messages from Ron.

I hurried to my car so that I could reply to his text. I didn't want him to get suspicious.

When I looked up, I saw that Lil was not at my car, she was walking with Melvin to his car. I yelled at Lil from my car and asked her where she was going. She said that Melvin wanted her to go with him. *Shoot, what about the remaining four rocks.* Even in that situation, I could only think about getting high. I yelled and asked her to come to my car for a moment. I walked to meet her halfway. When she was face to face with me, I asked her for two of the rocks that were left from the rocks she purchased earlier. She looked at me and said that she couldn't give them to me because she didn't think Melvin would give her anymore. I was shocked! We always shared our rocks, or at least I thought we did. I was also pissed. How dare she deny me after all I had gone through with her! I maintained my composure and simply said okay and walked away. She knew I was pissed. As I got in my car prepared to drive off, Lil came running to driver side window and handed me all four rocks. She said nothing and walked away. Before I pulled off, I replied to Ron's text and headed home.

When I got home, I took a shower and threw my clothes, including my bra and panties, into the washer. I took a nice hot shower, put on my favorite flannel pajamas and escaped to the guest room to finish off the four rocks. It was around eight o'clock that evening when I had finished up the four rocks and was sitting on the floor in the guest room zoned out. While I relaxed and savored the moment, the house phone started ringing. I did not answer it, because I did not want to be removed from my current state. It stopped ringing for about ten seconds, and then it started ringing again. I jumped up from the guest room and ran into my master bedroom to answer the phone. It was Michael looking for Lil. *Shit*, I thought to myself, *what can I tell him.*

"Hey Sam."

"Hi Michael. How are things going?" "Things here in India are going better than we expected. Hey, is Lil there? I've been calling the house and her cell, and she has not answered either one of them."

"She left here about ten minutes ago. She said her phone was dead, and she needed to charge it. She was not feeling well and said she was going home to take some Nyquil and go to bed. She is probably asleep, and I bet she didn't charge her phone up before she got in the bed."

"Well, she is not answering the house phone either."

"I will go and check on her and have her call you."

"Thanks Sam. That would be great if you can do that," Michael stated in a tone that was a mixture of suspicious and worried.

"Sure, no problem."

I hung up the phone, grabbed my keys, ran to the garage, got in my car, and headed toward Melvin's house. When I arrived at Melvin's house, it was dark and looked as if nobody was there. I rang the doorbell and waited for someone to come to the door, but no one answered. I banged on the door. Still, no one answered. I did that for about five minutes, and then got back in my car and went home. During my drive home, I constantly dialed Lil's number, but it went straight to voicemail. I could not help but begin to worry. I didn't know what Melvin had done with her. What would I tell Michael?

My house phone was ringing as I walked in the door. When I answered it, it was Michael again. I told him that I was just walking in the door after leaving his house. I told him that Lil didn't answer the door for me, so I used the spare key. I continued on with my made up story and told him that Lil was in the bed fast asleep and I did not want to wake her. I said that if she is not better in the morning, I would make her go to urgent care. As I was explaining this to him, someone in the background on his end was talking to him. He said he had to go, but asked me to tell Lil that he would check up on her in the morning, our time. I told him ok and hung up the phone. I dodged a bullet that time, but Michael is not dumb. I'm sure he wondered what was going on. I just hoped Lil got home soon.

CHAPTER 14

L il showed up at my door at six o'clock in the morning the next day. It was a blessing that Michael had not called yet. Lil was so high, and she reeked of alcohol and funk. She looked like she had not had a bath in days.

"Lil, what is going on with you? Where have you been? What did Melvin do to you?"

"That motherfucker didn't do anything to me. He had me ride around with him all night while he collected his fees. He got mad with me and said, 'If you want to ruin yourself by smoking crack, go ahead.' Then, he placed three eight balls in front of me and told me to have at it. I smoked as much as I could, but I was so high. I thought I was overdosing. I think that was Melvin's intent. He is so mad at me. I told him I smoked it all so he wouldn't take the rest. I was getting scared because my heart felt like it was going to come out of my chest. So I just laid myself back in his car while he went to multiple places to pick up his money. I dozed off... I actually think I blacked out. He couldn't wake me, so he got scared and dropped me off at my house. He put me in the back seat of my car.

That is when I woke up and asked him what the fuck he was doing. He said he couldn't get me to respond so he wanted me to be home so no one would have to find me with a crack dealer."

"That is some bullshit Lil! He was going to leave you in your car to die without calling for any help. That's a low down dirty dog."

"I know. After I cursed him out, I didn't even go in the house. I jumped in my car and drove here. I tried to be as quiet as I could so that I would not wake up the neighbors."

"You look awful! Michael has been calling here for you. He said he was going to call you this morning. I told him you were not feeling well and that I used the spare key to go check on you since there was no answer on the home or cell phones."

"Thanks Sam. Oh, and by the way, I apologize for trying to slight you the other day. I was not thinking clearly. You know I will always share with you."

"You had me wondering. You know, I really wish we never tried this crack. It really has changed us both. I have to find a way to get off of it. It's going to ruin my life. Hell, it is already ruining our lives!"

"No it's not Sam! You are so dramatic." "Lil, you are on probation at your job. We were held hostage in a crack house. Melvin now knows that both of us smoke crack, and his buddies Que and the big burly guy saw us there. Our cover is blown!"

"We are going to be just fine. We have to maintain control."

"So, is that what happened tonight? You maintained control while your lover dropped you off in the back seat of your car for dead!"

"Drama Queen! You are so over the top!" "What! What the fuck are you saying, Lil?

None of the stuff I just mentioned happened? You are the one who is in denial!"

"Whatever."

"What the fuck ever back at you! You need to take your funky ass upstairs, take a shower, and be present when Michael calls."

Lil stormed by me and intentionally stomped her way up my stairs to the guest room. I yelled up at her and told her to come back down and put her clothes that she had on in the washer and that I would bring her some fresh clothes. She said she has some clothes in the closet in the guest room and she would wear those. As soon as I heard the shower go on, the phone rang. I ran upstairs to my bedroom, grabbed the phone, and answered it. It was Michael, and he was very worried. I stopped him in mid-sentence and told him that Lil was here and that I would get her. I put the phone on mute and went to the bathroom door and told Lil it was Michael.

Luckily, she had not gotten in the shower yet. She turned the shower off, opened the door slightly, and grabbed the phone from me. As I was walking away, I could hear her fake coughing and telling Michael that she is feeling terrible and decided to come back to my house because she could not stand being home alone. I stood at the top of the steps to listen some more. Lil is a good actress, she put on a major show for him. All I could do was laugh as I went down the stairs.

***

Michael and Ron arrived back in town the following week. They cut their trip short because, while in India, they were able to obtain the funding needed to get their new venture off the ground and begin hiring employees. Lil and I didn't expect them back so soon. Therefore, we had to tread very carefully so that we would not be caught. The next morning, Ron woke up early and went to the gym. He told me that he was also meeting Michael for breakfast so that they could finalize some numbers on the deal that they were offered in India. During breakfast, Michael confided in Ron about Lil's strange behavior. He told Ron that he and Lil went out to dinner the first night they got back from India.

Since the kids were gone, he wanted to have a romantic evening with Lil. He made reservations at their favorite restaurant called the Inn at Little Washington, located in Washington, Virginia.
Lil loved to go to there, and he wanted it to be a surprise. It is approximately an hour and a half from the Washington, D.C. area. When she visited for the first time, she was so enamored with its charm and quaintness that she did a lot of research on the town of Washington and read thousands of reviews of the Inn at Little Washington. She was intrigued by its history.

She found out that many people refer to The Inn at Little Washington as a romantic fantasy world far removed from the harsh realities of modern- day life. For some, the culinary experience alone is the main reason to venture away from the city to this small town for dinner. As for the town of Washington, VA, per Lil, the historic Town of Washington was founded in 1769 and surveyed by George Washington. Many of the buildings date back to the late 1700s. In addition, there are art galleries, sophisticated shops, and theaters that Lil asked me to visit with her.

Michael confided in Ron about Lil's behavior at the restaurant. He said that he was so embarrassed by her actions. She kept saying the folks at the table that was next to theirs was staring at her. When he told Lil that they were just enjoying their dinner and not even looking at them, she seemed to get upset and began to raise her voice. He had to treat her as though he was handling a toddler or an elderly adult with Alzheimer's. He tried to hold her hands and gaze in her eyes, but she seemed on edge. They finished their dinner in peace, but Michael said the trouble came when they got in the car. The couple that Lil had accused of staring at her was also leaving. Michael went on to say that when they walked past his car, Lil jumped out and yelled at them, "Stop following me!"

At that moment, Michael jumped out of the car, went over to the passenger side where Lil was standing and shouting at the couple, and put his arms around her. He assured her that everything was ok, and they are not following her. He guided her into the front passenger seat and told her to put on her seat belt. Once Lil was in place and seemingly calm, he went over to the couple who was standing outside their car watching him and Lil. As he approached, they asked him if everything was ok. He answered them honestly and said that he didn't know. The male began to ask Michael about her behavior in more detail. Michael was actually stunned at the series of questions, and it must have shown on his face.

The male introduced himself as Stephen Myers, MD. He said he specializes in bipolar disorders. He asked how long had Lil been experiencing her episodes. Michael was confused and told Dr. Myers that he did not know what he meant about episodes. Dr. Myers explained that bipolar disorder is a condition that affects the brain in a way that can cause extreme mood swings that vary in length. People with bipolar disorder can go from mania, the "highs" - feeling euphoric or revved up and irritable, to depression, the "lows" - feeling down or hopeless. These highs and lows are called episodes. Michael explained to the Dr. that the only symptom he noticed lately was that she always felt like someone was following her or after her. Dr. Myers explained that Lil's symptoms could be part of the bipolar disorder, or it could be as sign of Schizophrenia. He asked Michael if it was ok if he talked to Lil. Michael agreed, and Dr. Myers went over to speak to Lil.

"Hello, my name is Stephen. I'm sorry if we upset you. We were just heading home and just happened to be going the same way. We are not following you. Ok?"

Lil seemed calm and asked him how he knew she would be there.

Dr. Myers explained that he didn't know and that nobody sent him. He said he and his wife were celebrating their fifth wedding anniversary. That seemed to make Lil feel a lot better. She apologized and told him she was just on edge and stressed out. He said he understood and walked back over to Michael. He told him that she needed to see a doctor. He gave Michael his card and said it could be stress, but it also could be something more serious. Michael took the card and thanked him. As he continued telling his story to Ron, Michael was almost in tears. He said Lil was just fine and acted as though nothing had happened when he got back into the car. He said he was worried about her. He wanted her to get checked out by the doctor, but he thought bringing it up at that time might make things worse.

Thankfully, ever since that night, he had not noticed anymore paranoia. He said that she seemed fine except that she does not sleep well at night.

Later that night, while getting ready for bed, Ron asked me if I had noticed anything different about Lil. My heart started beating really fast. I felt as if I was going to have another panic attack. If I showed that I was having a panic attack, Ron would think that something was wrong and that I was hiding something. I got up and went to my dresser and pretended that I was looking for my flannel pajamas. I was actually taking deep breaths in and out as an attempt to get my breathing under control. While rummaging through my drawers, I responded to Ron telling him that I had not noticed any changes in Lil. I told him that she has lost a lot of weight due do the diet we are both on. He said he noticed her weight loss and that it was significant. He also said he noticed that I have lost a lot of weight, too.

He went on to ask if I had noticed any changes in her behavior. I stopped him and asked him what was going on. I told him that Lil is my best friend and that we are together just about every day. He finally confessed that Michael had confided in him during breakfast, and he was worried about Lil. I acted very shocked to hear this and told Ron that I had not experienced anything like that when Lil and I were together.

I suggested that maybe she is stressed out at the job and told him that she had been complaining about her boss a lot lately. He asked me to pay attention and let him know if I noticed any changes so that

Michael can get her some help if it is needed. I told him that I could try and help her if needed, but I didn't think we should mention it to Lil. He told me that my offer would be great except he told Michael that he would not tell me. Therefore, it would have to be between us. I agreed. However, I knew that I could not tell Lil about Michael's suspicion, because she would lose it. I had to determine how to talk to her without her yelling. Her behavior had become so sporadic that you never knew what to expect.

Ron also reminded me that he and Michael were going to be in California for the next two weeks and wanted me to keep a close eye on Lil for Michael. I told him that I would and that she could stay at our house while they were away. He was happy with that and said he would let Michael know. Once we finally got into bed after we finished the conversation about Lil's behavior, the phone rang. For some reason, I was very nervous. I thought that it was Michael saying that Lil was not home and wondering if she was with us. Fortunately, it was Sam and Ronda. We put them on speaker, and they were both trying to compete with each other to tell us about the fun they were having. They tag- teamed on providing their updates.

Ronda gave us blow by blow of the fun that she and Michele were having at the day camp they attended. She said that they would go to the mall on the weekend. My brother's daughter, Trinity, was hanging out with them as well. Sam chimed in and said that he and Michael, Jr. went to the day camp, too. They did cool things like play basketball and baseball. He said they also went hiking. After they finished with their updates, we asked them if they were ready to come home. In unison they both said, "No." We told them that we would try not to let that hurt our feelings. They said they loved us, and we gave them our love. Then, we asked them to put Grandma on the phone. My mother took the phone and greeted us in her most cheerful voice. I teased her and said for a woman with four kids working her nerves, she sure sounded happy. As usual, my mother gave me another unsolicited mini lecture.

"You see, Samantha, when you practice patience and directness, the kids will do what they are told. Then, you will have no problem out of them."

"Yes Ma'am," is all I could say.

Ron chimed in and said, "How's my favorite most beautiful lady in the world doing today?"

"Oh Ronald! You get me every time."

She began giggling. My mother has always loved Ron. He could do no wrong in her eyes. If I was having a bad day and said something about Ron not helping me or not understanding, she would always take his side. I couldn't win with her when it came to Ron.

***

I arrived to work early the next day.

Monday mornings were always hectic, and I must admit that I had not been as focused as usual. I had made numerous errors with the contracts and even mixed the meetings up.

Fortunately, I caught the mistake before Daniel found out about it. It was around 6:30 a.m., and I was the only person in the office. At least I thought I was. As I sat at my desk proofreading the contract for security services, I heard some slight moaning coming from my boss's office. I thought I was imaging things because the lights were off and he did not usually arrive in the office until around 9:30 a.m. Furthermore, I didn't see his car in his reserved parking spot. I thought that maybe I was hearing things so I started back at proofreading the contract.

Suddenly, I heard more moaning. It was a man's deep groan along with a woman's high pitch scream. I jumped up and ran to Daniel's door and slowly opened it. I wanted to see who was in his office having sex without interrupting them. Once I had the door opened enough to see what was going on, I was totally shocked. My boss was fucking the shit out of whoever was underneath him. He had her bent over in doggie style with her hands on his desk and her ass sticking up and out. Her head was down, but from the hairstyle, it looked like Logan, the admin that covered for me when I dropped the kids in South Carolina during my two-week vacation. I couldn't believe it. Daniel was into black women?

His wife is white and Irish, and so is Daniel. I'm really shocked that he of all people liked to dip in the chocolate. As I watched Daniel bang and pound on poor Logan, she looked as though she could not handle the thrusts that he gave her. He would slow down and then speed up and bang her so hard that I had to shutter.

She was not giving it back to him. She should have been moving her ass back and forth as he thrust harder and harder. When Daniel pulled his penis out of the lady, he told her to suck it. That is when I got confirmation that it was indeed Logan. I also got a good glimpse at how huge Daniel's penis was. Damn, he was bigger than Ron! It was really large. I could see why Logan was screaming out in pain. It looked like his penis was longer than a ruler. I never would have imagined that he had that much to offer. I pushed the door open, and they both jumped up.

"Maybe next time, you two should lock the door and make sure no one else is in the office."

I walked out, slammed the door, and sat at my desk. A few minutes later, Logan come out looking like she just arrived at work. She was well put together. She looked at me, and I gave her the look of shame and went back to proofreading the contract. About thirty minutes later, the intercom buzzed. It was Daniel. I knew he wanted to talk about what I had just seen, but I was not in the mood. I didn't answer, so he buzzed again. I still didn't answer. He slowly walked out of his office, looked at me, and I looked back at him. He turned around, went back into his office, and closed the door. He didn't say anything to me the remainder of the day. I let him know when he had a call and who was calling. I gave him his calendar for the next day, but I did not go over it with him like I usually did. I decided to treat it like it never happened.

At ten o'clock, I got a call from Lil. She asked me to come down to the garage where she was parked. She said that it was urgent. I got up and left without telling Daniel that I was stepping away. I didn't think it would be a problem today. When Logan noticed that the phone was ringing and not being answered, she would answer. When I got to Lil's car, she had a box with her personal belongings in it.

"Hey Lil. What's up? You cleaning out your office."

"No girl. I was fired."

"Fired? Lil, you are shitting me." "Because of my absence from work or showing up at twelve or two in the afternoon. Taking lunch when I'm that late is the main reason for my termination. They said the numerous occasions this happened, and I didn't even call to let anyone know of my tardiness was the deciding factor."

"What are you going to do, Lil? You can't let Michael know. He will know something is up. He already thinks that you should get some help."

"What do you mean he thinks I should get some help?"

Shoot! I didn't mean to let that slip. I was going to have to tell Lil about Michael's suspicions.

"Lil, you have to promise to not say nothing to Michael. If you say something, then Ron will never tell me anything again."

"What is it, Samantha? What did Michael say about me?"

"Well, apparently, when you guys went out to dinner the other night at your favorite spot, you had one of your episodes of paranoia. You attacked a couple and told them to stop following you. The guy that you yelled at was a doctor and thinks you were having a bipolar episode. He convinced Michael that you needed to see a doctor for help."

"Aww shit, Sam! I did lose it. They kept staring at me when we were in the restaurant eating. Michael told me that they were not thinking about me and minding their business, but I swear I couldn't enjoy myself because of their stares. When Michael and I left, I looked up, and they were right there. I knew they were following me then. I yelled at them to stop. They just stood there looking at me like I was crazy. Michael came over to my side and comforted me, helped me back in the car, and put my seatbelt on me. He then went over to talk to the couple. They were over there talking for a while. Then, the guy came over and apologized. His ass should have been sorry."

Listening to Lil talk made me even more nervous. She really had it bad. It was getting worse. To top it off, she had lost her job. What was she going to do all day while everyone else was working? I knew the answer to that question which worried me even more. Lil promised that she would not mention anything to Michael and that she would leave out the house every morning like she was going to work. Luckily, Michael and Ron would be out of town for the next two weeks, so she did not have to worry since the kids would still be in South Carolina.

She could sleep in, but I knew better than that. Lil would be smoking crack all day. I just hoped she stayed away from Melvin.

CHAPTER 15

Ron was up early. He and Michael were headed to California to finalize all the details with the deal they landed a few weeks ago. They scheduled a limo service to pick them up. The limo driver would pick Michael up first, and then swing by to get Ron. When they used this limo service, the driver usually showed up in a black Lincoln Town car. As I helped Ron pack the last of his items, the driver was knocking at the door. I kissed him goodbye, and he was out the door. I watched as he loaded his luggage into the trunk and got in the back of the car. Michael was in the front. I continued to watch as the driver slowly backed out of the driveway and pulled onto the street. I felt an overwhelming since of sadness come over me. I needed a hit.

I went into the house to get ready for work. I really didn't feel like going in, but I was playing hard ball and doing whatever I wanted since I caught Daniel in the compromising position with Logan. When Logan would see me coming, she would go the other way or pretend that she was on the phone to avoid facing me. Daniel was so cool with it, and he acted like nothing happened. When he asked me to do something, he stared me down. It's like he enjoyed the fact that I knew he had sex with a black woman, and that maybe he could taste some of my sweetness. I hoped I was imagining this, but he sure had been staring me down. I think he knew that I saw how huge his dick was. I have to admit that I was getting a little wet as I watched them.

When I arrived at work, there was a note on my computer screen from Daniel. It read, "Come see me as soon as you get in." Damn, I thought to myself, I don't feel like being bothered with him today. I knew I should have stayed home. I knocked on Daniel's door, and he instructed me to enter. I slowly walked in and sat down in one of the wooden chairs that sat in front of his desk. I didn't say a word. I just stared at him directly in his eyes. He stared back at me, not intimidated at all. He finally broke the stare and asked me if I was going to say good morning. He went on to say that I walked into his office, sat down, and didn't have the decency to speak. I still did not utter one word to him.

Daniel leaned back in his chair and begin to speak. All I could think of while he was speaking was how hard he was pumping on Logan. As I snapped myself out of it, I focused back on Daniel talking. He said that I need to get past what I saw and not let it impact my choices and work performance. I lost it when he said that.

I yelled at the top of my voice, "How the hell do you expect me to get past what I saw, Daniel? I come into the office early to finish up some work for you, and you are in here banging the hell out of Logan. What kind of example is that? You disgust me. What about your wife and kids? You didn't even have the decency to wear a condom. You don't know where Logan has been nor does she know where you have been."

"You are not my mother, Samantha!" Daniel bellowed.

It startled me, because he had never talked to me in that tone.

"You work for me, and what I do with my personal life is none of your fucking business."

"It is my business if I come in and see you fucking the assistant!"

"Who I fuck and when I fuck them has nothing to do with you. You need to lose the attitude and do your job. That is why you are here, Samantha. Not to tell me who and when I fuck. You act like you are my wife. What, are you jealous, Samantha? Are you mad that it wasn't you that I had bent over on the desk fucking you like a whore? I always wanted to fuck a black woman and fuck her like a slave. That's what I did to Logan! Yeah, I said it. I fucked her like a slave and made her submit to me. I would never treat my white chicks like that. You black women deserve it."

Before I knew it, I was up out of my chair and beating the fuck out of Daniel. I picked up the book end on his credenza and hit him in the head with it. He jumped up and tried to restrain me. I got loose and started swinging, and he grabbed my hands. I lifted my feet and kicked him in his balls so hard that I know I damaged something. Daniel fell to the floor screaming in pain. That's when security came through the door to see what the commotion was. Once Daniel saw the officers, he instructed them in a weak voice to have me removed from the office immediately. He was still laying on the floor holding his private area, but he was able to raise his head and tell me that I was fired.

I walked out and yelled, "Great, I could not work for a racist son of a bitch like you anyway!"

Security followed me to my desk and waited for me to get my belongings. While I was packing up my things, Logan came by to see what was going on. I told her to walk with me to my car. She looked nervous. I told her it was ok and that I was not mad at her, but I really needed to talk to her. Once we got to the front of the building, security sent me on my way. Logan and I continued to walk out to the parking lot to my car. Once we got there, I put my belonging in my trunk and asked Logan to get in. She sat in the front, and I told her why I was fired. I told her everything that Daniel said about having sex with her and how he used her and had all intentions of just fucking her like a slave. She began to cry and told me that was how she felt. She said he ordered her to do crazy things.

She went on to say that was their fifth time having sex. She said she didn't want to have sex with him, but he kept threatening her job so she gave in to his advances. She said he treated her very bad and would call her his slave while she was having sex with him. She began to cry hysterically. I told her she needed to sue.

Suddenly, I got an idea of how to get some money for crack. I would have Lily tell Melvin what happened and get his boys to beat Daniel's ass and blackmail him for money. It was time to put a plan in action, since I had lost my job, was addicted to crack, had limited funds, and, if I wanted to keep my addiction away from my husband. I dropped Logan back off at the front of the building and called Lil. To my surprise, she answered the phone on the second ring.

"Girl, you are not going to believe what just happened to me!"

"What?" Lil asked groggily.

"Why does your voice sound muffled? Where are you?" I asked, knowing what she was doing.

"I'm home, downstairs in the guest room." "You got some?"

"Yup," she replied.

"Where'd you get it? Melvin?" "Yup."

"I'm on my way."

"Good, you taking off work early?"

"That's what I need to tell you. I was fired." Her voiced cleared when she heard that.

"What! Not you Sam, what the hell happened?" "Well, remember when I told you about me walking in on Daniel and Logan having sex? Wait, let me change that, remember when I told you about waking in on Daniel and Logan fucking?"

"Yes."

"Well, I have not said anything to Daniel or Logan since then. Today when I got in, there was a note on my computer from Daniel to come in his office when I got in. I was instantly pissed. I went in, sat down, and didn't say a word. He stared me down, and I stared him down, too. He finally broke the silence and told me that I am not his mother. But, here is the crazy part. He told me that I was mad, and that he always wanted to fuck a black woman and treat her like a slave, and that is what he did to Logan."

"Wait! What the fuck are you saying? He called you a slave, and he called Logan a slave and that he treated her like that?"

"Yes! He even said he would never treat his white women like that! At that point, I jumped up and attacked him. I was so mad. I was swinging and kicking on him. I finally got him good. I kicked him as hard as I could right in the balls. I know I damaged something. I talked to Logan, and she told me he treated her so bad. She said he called her slave and made her do things that she was too embarrassed to share. She said he threatened to fire her if she did not do it. She said she needed the job to care for her son."

"That son of a bitch is going to pay. I like Logan. She is a nice girl. I always thought so until you told me about them fucking, but now I know why," Lil replied.

"Daniel needs to pay for this. I'm not even mad about losing my job. I'm mad because I've been working for a racist asshole for all these years. He's a great actor. I have an idea, but I will discuss it with you when I get there. I'm almost there. I will talk to you in a few."

I hung the phone from talking to Lil and that is when everything hit me all at once. I started bawling. I couldn't stop the flow of tears. All I could ask myself was how did I get in that situation. How was I going to hide that I'm not working from my husband? This is so crazy. I did all of that to lose weight. I lost weight, but my life was in shambles. I wanted to smoke crack, because I liked how it makes me feel. However, I don't want to deal with the consequences. Who would do some stupid shit like this anyway? I knew smoking crack was crazy. However, I thought that since I was an intelligent, educated, and well-raised woman, I would not be affected by the crack. I figured that I would get through the two months having lost twenty pounds and everything would go back to normal. I would feel good about myself and would believe that my husband was really attracted to me. Although he has never given me a reason to think he was interested in a smaller framed woman, I never quite felt like I measured up. Boy, did I screw up.

When I arrived at Lil's, she was downstairs in the guest room. I rang the doorbell at least ten times, but she did not answer. I had to use the spare key she gave me in case of an emergency. I only used it this time because I knew she was home alone. As I entered the room, Lil was in the midst of her paranoia episode. She was looking out the window and didn't see me enter the room. When I spoke, she screamed so loud that you would have thought I had a gun in my hand or something. She then ran out of the room and checked the other rooms and closed the doors. When she came back in the room, she started asking me who was with me. I told her that I was by myself, but she had to recheck the rooms again before she felt safe. Once she settled down, I needed a hit bad. I grabbed her pipe and asked her for a piece of rock to put in it to smoke. Lil gave me a look as though I had lost my mind.

"Oh, you don't have your own?" she asked with an attitude.

"No, Lil, I don't have my own. I thought you were the one who would get it for me. Has that changed? You are starting that same shit up again that you pulled when you dragged me to that damn crack house."

I was annoyed. She was now questioning me about smoking her crack? We always shared. I was really pissed off. Lil looked at me and gave me a guilty gesture by hunching up her shoulders and poking out her lips.

"Here, take this, but we are going to have to go out and get some more soon. This time you pay for it. I'm not going to ask Melvin for nothing. Bastard! Left me out for dead, and now he's been calling me to come over to talk. So we may have to go back to the crack house we visited."

"Absolutely not! I am not going back over there," I assured her.

"Sam, they know that I'm Melvin's girl, so either they will call him or just give me what I want."

I suggested that we smoke what she had and make the decision then. I put a rock into the pipe and inhaled deeply. I was in desperate need for this hit. About fifteen minutes after my hit, I gave Lil blow by blow of what went down with Daniel. I was infuriated all over again just by rehashing the scene. Lil was very upset.

Moreover, she was high as hell which took it to another level. She wanted to go back to the office, flatten his tires, and then go to his house to tell his wife what happened and how her husband liked black women. I calmed her down and told her that going back to the office was a bad idea. I really wanted Lil to convince Melvin to get his boys to beat Daniel's ass, and then blackmail him for money. However, since Lil was pissed off with Melvin, I didn't think it was a good time to bring it up.

Suddenly, as if Lil read my mind, she said, "We need to get somebody to kick his ass. I mean really fuck him up, Sam."

"What do you have in mind, Lil?"

At this point, I was jumping for joy in the inside, but, I had to play it cool so Lil would not suspect that this was my plan all along. Lil said that she could contact Melvin by returning his calls. She would go and have a talk with him to smooth things over, get some more crack, and then she would tell him about what Daniel did to me. She said once Melvin knew what Daniel said about treating black women as slaves, he would lose his fucking mind. I was all in. Except there was one thing Lil left out.

"Lil, the plan sounds great, but there is one thing I don't understand.

"What's that?"

"How do you expect Melvin to give you more crack and come to your defense, well really, my defense, if you don't fuck him?"

"Oh, I know I have to fuck him again. It will be over by the time I blink my eyes."

"Are you sure, Lil?"

"Wow Sam! I can't believe you. You have such double standards. At first you were preaching to me to leave Melvin alone and asking me what about my husband and kids.

Now that this benefits you, I didn't hear a word. I'm starting to wonder about you, Sam. Are you really my best friend?"

"It's not like that, Lil. I promise. I still don't think you should be fucking with Melvin, but I would prefer we go to him to get our crack instead of that crack house. Plus, I really do think that Daniel needs to get fucked up for what he said to me. We really need Melvin right now. Although I don't agree with the situation, we are both in too deep, and we have to find a way to get out."

Lil listened intently to what I was saying, and I could tell that she knew I was right and that I did really have her best intentions in mind. I just didn't want to go back to that crack house. Lil picked up her cell phone and called Melvin. When he answered the phone, Lil placed the call on speaker phone, looked at me, and gestured for me to be quiet. Meanwhile, I took another hit. Once I finished my long inhale and slow exhale, I listened to Melvin apologize for how he treated Lil. He was begging for her to come over so he could make it up to her. He told her he had a ball for her and that he missed her loving. He told Lil to bring me with her so that he could apologize to me as well. I thought that was a nice gesture. I had to make things right with him so he didn't tell Ron about my new endeavors.

About an hour after Lil got off the phone with Melvin, we were pulling up to his house. There were no cars in the driveway or parked on the street in front of Melvin's house like it usually was. I felt relieved because that meant there was less chance of someone seeing me and telling Ron. When Lil and I got to the door, we didn't even have to ring the doorbell. It seemed to automatically open. When we stepped inside, the big burly guy from the crack house was the one who had opened it for us. He had to be watching us the entire time. Lil asked him where Melvin was, and he told her to go downstairs. Lil started to say something, but he grabbed her by her arms, shoved her forward, and forced her down the steps. Suddenly, I felt someone brush up against the back of me. As soon as I turned to see what was going on, my hands were grabbed, and I was also forced down the stairs. When we got downstairs, Melvin was lounging on the sectional sofa in his basement. There were two other women there who were naked and sitting on the opposite side of the couch.

They looked like this was a norm for them. Melvin ordered the guys who were holding Lil and me captive to let us go. He then proceeded to tell us the rules.

"Nobody disrespects me. When you disrespect me, you must pay. Your payment is to be gang fucked so that you will know to never cross Melvin."

Lil chimed in and asked Melvin what was he talking about. She started screaming at him, "Nobody disrespected you Melvin! You disrespected me by leaving me in my car for dead! Then, you lure me over here to be abused by you and your boys. I'm not that kind of woman. I think you must have me mistaken for one of your tricks."

Melvin began to laugh and then applauded Lil, saying that her performance was Oscar status. Lil went over to him and smacked him.

Melvin jumped up, grabbed Lil, and forced her into one of the rooms in the basement. Before he closed the door, he told the two guys that he would have his way with Lil, and then they could come in once he was done. He also went on to say that they should start with us ladies that were in the basement - that included me. Oh no, I needed to get out of there. That's when the big burly guy pointed at me and said that he wanted me. He grabbed me from behind and forced me into another room.

Once we were in the room, he instructed me to remove my clothes. I stood there and didn't move. He grabbed the front of my blouse and ripped it open. Then, he raised my bra up so that my nipples would show. He began to fondle my nipples. He removed his pants and underwear while he was standing in front of me watching my every move. He penis was fully erect and waiting for some action. I thought to myself, there is no way this fool is going to put that in me. I don't know where it's been, and I don't want no parts of it. I had to find a way out. I began to inch back closer and closer to the door as he continued to play with my nipples.

Suddenly, I heard a loud scream. The big burly guy ran past me and opened the door. As I trailed behind him, I saw Lil running from the room buck-naked and heading towards the door. I ran behind her, and we jumped in the car. Lil got behind the wheel, cranked it up, and skidded away. She was driving so fast, but I was glad because we had to get away. I told Lil to go to my house because Melvin would probably send someone to her house.

"What did you do, Lil?"

"I bit it," she said as she tried to catch her breath.

"You bit what?"

"I bit his fucking dick!"

"Oh My God! Did you take if off? What do you mean you bit it?

"I didn't take it off, but I bit it enough so that he would have pain and would not be able to use if for a while. I couldn't believe he would disrespect me like that? I had to teach him a lesson."

"Lil, do you know what you've done? He's going to come after us.

"No he isn't. He thinks that I will be back to get more crack from him. I will just go somewhere else. I'm done with Melvin - for good this time.

"I can't believe he set us up. I thought he wanted to apologize to me. He had this planned all along. What a bastard!"

"No worries, he will get his. Trust me.

Now, I have to find another way to get crack. Oh shoot. I just remembered that I have a number for one of Melvin's boys. All I have to do is text him what I want, and he will tell me where to meet him. The thing is, you will have to get it because he knows me from being with Melvin, and he will tell Melvin where I am.

"I don't want to go on no strip to get no drugs, Lil."

"You don't have to go on the strip. You just send a text of what you want, and he will reply with where to meet him at."

"I'm not feeling comfortable with this, but I guess if we want to get an eight tonight, this is the only way."

"I think we should lay low tonight.

Actually, let's swing by the crack house that we went to last time. There were people out front selling."

We went to my house. I'm glad we had my car, because we were able to pull in the garage so the neighbors would not see us with no clothes on. It also helped that my windows were tinted. We changed clothes, and then jumped back in my car. This time, I was driving and heading to the crack house that we frequented before. When we got there, just as Lil stated, there were guys out front hanging out. We saw them make a quick deal. I drove by slowly. Lil and I had on baseball hats to disguise our looks. When the young kid walked up to my car, he asked what I was looking for. I told him an eight. He reached in his pocket and showed me twelve bags of crack. I gave him $200 and pulled off.

I handed the bags of crack to Lil and asked her to taste one to make sure it wasn't soap this time. Lil said it was crack. I was relieved. After a night of almost being raped and being fueled with anger over being called a slave, I needed to unwind. I couldn't wait to get home so I could dive into my crack and allow it to take me to another world.

We made it back to my house safely. I locked the doors, turned out the lights, and we headed upstairs to the guest room. I went into my master bedroom to get the phone just in case Ron called. I didn't want to miss his call and have any unnecessary drama. We had enough of that going on now. When I entered my guest room, Lil had already assumed her position on the floor with her pipe in hand and inhaling away. I sat across from her on the floor and began my ritual of placing the crack on my homemade pipe. It worked wonders, and I got the best high from that pipe. I inhaled and let the crack take me to another place. I closed my eyes and let my mind wander. All I could think about was Daniel. How dare he call me a slave and want to fuck black women so he can get the opportunity to treat them as a slave. I wish Logan would have bit the fuck out of his dick just as Lil did Melvin's. I bet he would not have been able to abuse another black woman. Then, I began to think about Logan. I really felt sorry for her. Logan is about ten years younger than I am, so that would make her around thirty-two years old. I reached for my cell phone to call and check on her.

"Hello."

"Hi Logan. This is Sam. How are you doing?"

"Sam! I'm so glad to hear from you. I have been looking for your number. I need to talk to you ASAP, and I can't talk over the phone. I'm afraid that something bad has happened."

"What is it, Logan? Why can't you talk over the phone? What's going on?"

"Sam, I really need to come see you. I can't talk over the phone."

"Is it about Daniel? What is it? Tell me something, Logan," I pleaded.

"It's not about Daniel, but it is very urgent that I see you now."

Logan sounded like she was crying. I told her to come over, and I asked her if it was ok if Lil was here. I told her that she was spending the weekend with me since our husbands were out of town. Logan said it was fine, and she arrived at my house about twenty minutes after we ended our call. She knew where I lived because she came by on numerous occasions to drop some items off that Daniel needed me to work on after hours. I opened the door and guided her to the family room. Lil was still upstairs in the guest room. She would come down when she was ready. I offered Logan some coffee. She declined but asked if I had tea. I told her to have a seat while I went into the kitchen to fix her tea. Instead of taking a seat, Logan followed me in the kitchen. As I put the tea kettle on for her hot water, Logan began to sob uncontrollably.

"What is it Logan? What's wrong?"

"Sam, I messed up real bad. He's dead, Sam! He's really dead!" she cried.

"Who's dead? What are you talking about?"

"Daniel! I got my brother to go and rough him up for what he did to me. My brother said it got out of control. He said when he approached Daniel and asked him about treating black women like slaves, Daniel got real indignant with him. He said that Daniel told him to bend over and he would treat him like a slave just like he treated that stupid bitch that he rammed numerous times. My brother lost it and shot him in the head execution style. He's dead, Sam!'

"Wow Logan… I wasn't expecting to hear that. I just have one question for you. Why are you crying over that motherfucker? He deserved everything he got," I said nonchalantly.

"What if the police tie everything together and find out that I was involved with getting him killed?

"Don't you worry about that. We can be each other's alibi."

At that moment, Lil came down the stairs.

She caught the end of the conversation, so we had to fill her in with all of the details. Lil began laughing uncontrollably. Logan and I just stared at her. I knew that she was high, but Logan probably thought that she was drunk. When she finally stopped laughing, she jumped up and went into a rant.

"How dare that motherfucker disrespect a black queen. How dare he treat you like trash and ruin your dreams and womanhood. He took a gentle soul and made her hard core. Finding love again will be hard for you, my child," Lil said as she turned to face Logan. "He took something precious and you need to heal from the inside out. Our ancestors had to grow up protecting men who hated them but used them to rape and degrade them. It's awful. How dare he treat you like that. How dare you not to fight back. He had you scared of losing your job, but you lost so much more. I will spit on his grave."

Tears began to run down Lil's face.

Minutes later, tears began to flow from Logan's eyes, and then mine. We all began to cry uncontrollably. I mean that ugly cry. We all have done the ugly cry before. This was definitely the right moment for it. Lil's speech touched us deeply. It also made us realize that the struggle was not over. We were still facing racism, even with a black president. Hell, it seems as though racism had gotten worse since President Obama was elected to office.

All I could say was, "Lord help us. We need you now more than ever before."

Lil, Logan, and I devised a plan for when the cops come to us for questioning. We would say we were all together and that we had a girls' movie night at the house. I told Logan to stay the night so people would see her leave my house and also see her car parked out front.

Later that night, Logan got a call from her brother. He told her that he and his boys disposed of Daniel's body and no one would ever find it. No one asked any questions. It felt as though we had a sense of sadness, but at the same time, a sense of peace. It was not right, but that's how it felt.

I sent Logan upstairs to freshen up. I told her to sleep in Ronda's room because the guest room needed some work, and it was off limits.

After Logan finished her shower, she said that she was exhausted and that she was going to go to bed. Her son was at his father's house for the weekend, so she didn't have to worry about his well-being at the time. When Logan closed the door to Ronda's bedroom, Lil and I quietly went back into the guest room and smoked crack all night. Logan did not wake up at all. She was worn out with carrying the heavy burden about Daniel's death on her shoulders.

The next morning, news about Daniel missing was all over the news. The headlines read, CEO of SLICO Advertising Missing. Daniel's wife did an interview and said that she had just talked to him and asked him to pick up milk on his way home, but he never made it home. She went on to explain that he was a great husband and father, and he was very predictable with his habits. I couldn't help but laugh out loud. If only she knew how unpredictable he was. When Logan woke up and came downstairs, I turned to the news so she could hear the latest. She also got a chuckle out of Daniel's wife's statement. Lil did as well. Logan gave Lil and I a long and tight hug and thanked us for our help. She said she would call if she had any updates and that she would check in on me every once in a while. Lil and I both walked her out to her car. We wanted the neighbors to see her leaving just in case. As expected, Mrs. Lewis, my next door neighbor was out in her yard and waved hello to me. Alibi. Perfect.

CHAPTER 16

Ron and Michael's trip got extended for another two weeks. They were due home yesterday, but Ron called and said that there were still some things that needed to get finalized before he and Michael returned. He said it would probably be another two weeks, but it could be sooner. I was happy but I didn't want Ron to know it. I needed another two weeks to get myself together. I told him about Daniel being missing since it was on the news. He was shocked to hear that. I told him that I was told not to go into the office until further notice. Ron understood and said it is probably for the best since no one knows what happened, just in case he was involved in something illegal. I chuckled to myself and told Ron that I agree with him. The first thing he wanted to know was what I was going to do with my time. I told him I was going to go to the gym in the mornings and take some cooking classes. He was happy with that. I knew he was going to try and clock my time.

Lil had not been home since the incident at Melvin's house. She wanted to go home to check everything out and make sure the house was ok. I told her that I would go with her. We planned to arrive at Lil's house at one o'clock.

Most people are at work during that time, so if anyone showed up to harass us, the neighbors wouldn't be home to see it. We both were still very nervous. That incident with Melvin really shook us up something terrible. Before we headed to Lil's house, we were trying to figure out a way to get another eight. We had both maxed out our credit cards, and we were out of crack. I had exhausted all of the money in my bank account. If I went into the joint account, Ron would know something is up. Hell, I didn't even have a debit card for that account. That is the account he uses to pay the bills and manage the household expenses. I usually would just write a check when I went to the store. We were out of options. I needed to find a way to get some money.

Suddenly, I remembered that I paid for the last eight that we got, so Lil needed to pay this time. I told Lil that it was her turn to pay for the eight. She said she knew that and had a plan to get some money. She was ready to go to her house, so we left a little earlier than planned. It was eleven o'clock, but Lil's neighbors should still be at work. When we arrived at Lil's house, everything looked fine. There was no sign of Melvin or any of his groupies. When we entered the house, it looked fine as well. Lil said she didn't even receive any phone calls from Melvin after she bit him. Hopefully, that would make him leave us alone. In the meantime, we were still watching our backs.

Lil went to her bedroom and was in there for a while. When she came out, she was ready to go. I asked her where were we going and she stated to get the eight. She held up a handful of jewelry. I asked her if the guy would accept that, and she said probably not and that we were going to the pawn shop to get the money. When we arrived at the pawn shop, we sat in the car for a while to watch the customers that went to and fro. We wanted to make sure that there was no one that we knew and would report back to our husbands. When we entered the store, we saw all kinds of jewelry, electronics, instruments, and computers for sell. This was our first time visiting a pawn shop, so we didn't know what to expect.

The lady that was behind the counter was very helpful. Lil explained that she needed cash urgently and wanted to know how much she could get for the 18K gold necklace and diamond earrings. The lady asked if she wanted to sell it or pawn it. Lil didn't know what she meant, so she asked the lady what the difference was. The lady explained that pawning an item means that you are using your item as collateral to secure a loan. She said that after appraising the value of Lil's jewelry, they will work with her to determine the loan amount. She also explained that Lil would have to leave the jewelry with them until it's time for her to come back and repay the loan and collect her jewelry. She went on to say that if Lil decides to pawn and does not come back and repay the loan to get her jewelry, then it becomes the property of the pawn shop. She explained that selling the jewelry is just that. Lil would sell them the jewelry and the deal would be done.

Lil decided to pawn the jewelry because she did not want to lose the necklace that Michael gave her for their wedding anniversary a few years ago. The earrings were a gift he had given her for Valentine's Day last year. After the manager of the pawn shop inspected the jewelry, the lady bought the jewelry back to the counter and said that they would give her $1200 for both. Lil jumped at the deal. She had two months to pay the $1200 back, or it would be the property of the pawn shop. The lady placed the $1200 cash in Lil's hand, and we were out of there. Next stop, crack dealer.

***

As we approached the strip, it was not as busy as it was when we went there last night.

We did not think that visiting the strip in broad day light would pose a problem, but, it did.

There was nobody out on the street. Where was everybody? It looked deserted. We pulled over and parked across the street from the crack house that we visited a while back when we first met the big burly guy. We were going to wait until we saw someone come out of the crack house and see if they would help us make a purchase. We were sitting there watching the house for about ten minutes when Melvin suddenly pulled up. He and his boys jumped out of his Escalade and surrounded the car. Lil and I were so scared that we just froze and didn't move or say a word.

Melvin came to the window and demanded that I roll it down. I didn't move. His demand was much louder this time, but as I said, I was frozen. I didn't budge. That's when the big burly guy came over to the window and smashed it with his fist. I screamed. Glass shattered all over my lap, and some got into my hair. Melvin reached into the car and pressed the button that unlocks the door, opened the door, grabbed me out of the car, and pushed me toward the big burly guy. He then went to the passenger side where Lil was sitting and grabbed her. Lil began kicking and trying to fight Melvin, so he put his hands around her neck and told her that if she made another move, she was dead.

Lil stopped kicking and followed Melvin's orders. We were put in the back seat of his Escalade and driven back to his house. When we got inside of Melvin's house, we were guided downstairs just like last time. This time we were instructed to sit on the sofa in the basement. I was glad that we were not sent into the bedrooms like last time. Melvin was very angry. He bent down so that his face was right in front of us as we were sitting very close to each other. I guess we sat so close so that we could protect each other.

Melvin started yelling, "You two bitches think you got away? You done fucked up now. You don't know who you are messing with. I'm going to get you two so strung out, and then use you like a two-dollar ho. You don't fuck over me!"

He then put his hand around Lil's neck. "And you, you gone try and bite my dick off? You lucky you didn't cause any major damage, bitch, just some soreness. But, I'm going to fuck you until you are raw. I'll teach you to bite another motherfucker. You know, I really liked you too, Lil. You are nothing to me now. Both of yall's life is going to shit. I will make sure your husbands know that their precious wives are strung out on crack and getting gang banged every day. You think they will want you then? Fuck no! I am going to see to that! You fucking slut bitches!"

Melvin walked away and into one of the bedrooms. He came back with two syringe needles in his hand. He looked up and nodded at the big burly guy, who was sitting there the whole time while Melvin was on his rant. The guy jumped up, grabbed me, and held the needle up.

"Time to go to Lala Land."

I tried to get away, but Melvin grabbed my arms, and one of the other guys grabbed my legs. I could not move. The next thing I felt was like a surge of pleasure. It was a rush compared to no other. Even when I smoked crack, I didn't get a rush like that. I was floating and looking down on the men. It was a calming experience. After about twenty minutes, my mouth was dry and my limbs felt heavy like I couldn't lift my arms or move my legs at all. I was still very high from the dose I was given. They injected Lil with the same drug, and she put up a fight just as I did. It took the same three guys to hold her down while they injected her. Lil responded to the drug a little different from how I did. She was very hyper and just like the crack, she couldn't keep still. With this drug, she was not paranoid, just busy. The guys had left the room, and Lil and I were in the basement alone. I told her we needed to find a way to get out of there before we were raped. Melvin heard me talking to Lil about escaping, so he gave both of us another shot. This time, he filled the syringe all the way up. I was so high that I was experiencing shortness of breath. As I lost consciousness, I prayed to God that He would come rescue us.

When I woke up, I was butt naked in the same room where the big burly guy had me before. I was handcuffed to the bed, and he was standing at the foot of the bed with his penis in his hand. I began to scream. He slapped me and told me to shut the fuck up. I begged him not to rape me. I told him I had kids who were depending on me and that I would pay him whatever he wanted. Nothing I said mattered to him. He simply replied that he had what he wanted right in front of him. Then, he took his hands and spread my legs apart as wide as he could get them. He then pulled rope from the drawer where he was standing and wrapped the rope around each leg and tied it in a knot so that my legs were wide open. There was nothing I could do. I just silently wept and kept asking myself why did I let myself get in this position.

I'm not stupid, I knew what crack could do. I just thought it would not happen to me because I was in control and had a great life. I was so desperate to be thin that I ignored all of the logical thinking. Now look at me, I am addicted to crack and laying here being raped by a thug drug dealer. God, I swear if you get me out of this, I will definitely get some help. I will get help for Lil, too.

The big burly guy took some baby oil and squirted oil all over my vagina. He then put on a condom as he watched me with a smirk on his face. He put his heavy body on top of mine and thrust his penis inside me. I gasped and began to cry. There was nothing I could do but let him have his way. I could hear Lil's screams coming from the other room. It sounded like there were more guys in her room than just Melvin. My heart ached for her, and I knew that they would be in the room with me next. Shortly after the big burly guy finished, he got up, wiped himself off, and then knocked on the door. Two more guys entered the room.

"Ah yeah, I can't wait to fuck this bitch. Look at the ass on her. She don't even look like a crack ho bitch," one of the guys said with a sly smile.

All three of the guys began to laugh. The big burly guy gave one of the guys a thumbs up, and then left the room. The two guys looked as though they were in their early twenties. One was very slim and had his jeans hanging off his ass. The other guy had a medium build and was very light-skinned with dreads that were about shoulder length. My legs and arms were still restrained, so I had no power to fight. The only defense I could use was my voice. I began to talk to them.

"Please don't do this. I am old enough to be your mother. I just wanted to try crack to lose weight. I am not a crack head."

They both started laughing again and the very slim guy got on top of me and put his face very close to mine.

"You old enough to be my mother huh?

Well let me see how it feels to fuck my mother."

He unzipped his pants and pulled out his erect penis. He jammed it into me, and as he was fucking me, he was calling me all kinds of names.

"Bitch, I fucked my mama because she was a crack ho. Now I'm fucking you. Oh shit… Your pussy is much better than my mama's. You like it, don't you, bitch?"

He began to bang me harder and harder, all the while talking about how he fucked his mama. It seemed as though when he mentioned his mama, the angrier he got. He thrusted in and out of me with such intense power that my vagina was throbbing. I was in so much pain, but I refused to cry out loud. At this point, all I could think about was that I had to endure this one more time with the light-skinned guy. The slim guy finally finished. When he reached his orgasm, it was so intense, that it looked and felt as though he was having a seizure. Once he came to a stop with his convulsing, he jumped up and told the slim guy that it was his turn. As he was leaving the room, he made eye contact with me, looked down, and left the room.

Then, the light skinned guy pulled out his erect penis and got on top of me. Luckily for me, he was not large in size like the two before him. He entered my vagina, which was throbbing from pain and about two minutes later he was done. He jumped up and ran out of the room. A few minutes later the big burly guy entered. He un-cuffed my hands and untied my feet. He told me to get dressed and to come out to the main basement area when I was done. Once he left the room. I rolled over in a fetal position and began to cry uncontrollably. After about ten minutes of crying, I finally pulled myself together, got up, got dressed and went to the main room in the basement. My vagina was throbbing, and I could barely keep my balance. I was stumbling so bad that I accidentally bumped into the thin guy. He yelled at me to stand straight up. Then, he pushed me, and I fell onto the couch. I stayed there laid back with my head in my hands silently crying.

About ten minutes later, Lil was being guided out to the main room where I was thrown on the couch. Melvin had her by her hair and shoved her onto the couch where I was. She landed face first, and then sat up. She had a black eye and a busted lip that was swollen.

Melvin and the guys began talking about what to do with us. Melvin told the guys that they would have to get rid of us because we knew too much. Lil and I looked at each other, and we knew that we had to escape somehow, some way. As the men discussed how they were going to dispose of us, Lil reached over and whispered in my ear that she had a needle. I wasn't sure what she was saying, so I put a quizzical look on my face. She leaned back over and said that she had a needle that he had injected us with. I immediately knew what her plan was. When I leaned back over to ask her when she planned on using it, Melvin jumped up and yelled at us.

"No talking bitches! You two are going to see your last hours of life, so you better be thinking about good things before the darkness of death hits you."

The guys began talking again. Melvin said that they needed to kill us and dispose of our bodies in the early morning around 3 a.m. He told them that that was the best time and when the least of activity is going on. He reminded them to get rid of Lil and me just like they got rid of Sandy. I don't know who Sandy was, but I swore to God that I was going to fight with everything in me to get away. I kept having visions of my children and Ron. He was probably worried and put some sort of search and rescue out looking for me because I had not answered my phone in two days. Melvin instructed the big burly guy to go get my car from where they kidnapped us. He said to drop the car off in front of Lil's house and to keep the lights off so that no neighbors would see or hear him. When Melvin and his guys bum-rushed us, we left everything in my car including our purses. My keys were still in the ignition but the big burly guy had shut it off based on Melvin's instruction. It was about 1:00 a.m. and Melvin told the other two guys that it was time to dispose of us.

The two guys approached us. By then, we were now sitting very close to each other holding hands. They ordered us to get up as they both pointed a gun at the back of our heads and told us to walk slowly towards the car. The light- skinned guy with dreads threatened us by saying that if we made a sound or put up any type of resistance, he would shoot us both dead. Lil and I obliged and just looked at each other to try and communicate with our eyes. Before this crack shit, Lil and I were outstanding wives and mothers. We were always able to know what the other was thinking. I sure prayed that in this life-threatening situation, she was able to read my thoughts.

Once we were in the SUV, the slim guy was driving and the light skinned guy with dreads sat in the passenger seat facing us as we sat in the back seat. He had the gun pointed at us and continued to threaten that if we made one move, we would be dead sooner than planned. The windows on the SUV were tinted very black. In fact, it was tinted to such a dark tint that it was illegal. From the looks of it, the windows on this truck had to be about 80-90% VLT. In other words, you can't see out or in when looking through the tinted windows.

Thankfully, the two guys decided not to handcuff us. With the plan Lil briefly whispered in my ear while seated on the couch at Melvin's house earlier, not having our hands tied is a definite bonus. The only problem we had was determining how we were going to pull the needle out and stick it in the driver's neck if the light skinned guy was facing us with a gun pointed on us. Since Lil had the needle, she would be the one to pull it out. I just had to distract the guy with the gun.

After driving for about ten minutes, we came to a stop light. Lil and I exchanged glances to say that the time was now or never. I told the guy who was holding the gun that I felt like I was going to throw up. I began gagging and put my hand over my mouth like I was holding it in. My reaction startled the driver, and he swerved and pulled the SUV over to the shoulder. I could not open the door because the child safety locks were on, the guy with the gun had to open the door for me. Once his hand was on the lock, and I heard the door open, I pushed forward so hard that it knocked him down.

At the same time, Lil stuck the needle in the driver's neck. I grabbed the gun when I knocked the guy with the gun down and ran over to the passenger side to open the door for Lil. The driver jumped out of the SUV and grabbed Lil. I pointed the gun at him and told him to lay on the ground faced down.

Suddenly, the guy I knocked down came running from the other side of the SUV. I pointed the gun at him and ordered him down. Lil found a brick that was on the shoulder. She picked it up and started beating the guys in the head with the brick. I let her beat them in the head with the brick for about ten blows, and then I stopped her. I instructed Lil to turn them over so that they were laying on their backs.

Once they were in the position, I shot each one of them twice in the groin area. They let out the most awful screams. At that point, I knew Lil and I had to get out of there. She jumped in the passenger seat, and I jumped in the driver's seat. We drove that SUV to the drug strip where we left my car. It was still there intact.

Once we pulled up, the guys that were on the street selling their products, thought that we were Melvin. When they approached the car, Lil told them that she was instructed to come pickup two eights for Melvin. The guys did not give her any problem because she had his car. Lil told the guys that Melvin wanted to leave his car there and for them to watch it. She told them that he would be back in about two hours. They asked Lil why she was swapping cars and she told them that something went down and Melvin would tell them all about it.

For some odd reason, they believed her and went back to their area on the street that they claimed. Before we got out of Melvin's SUV, we wiped our fingerprints off the gun and the car using our blouse and then tossed the gun out the window into the wooded section. We slowly walked to my car so that we did not look suspicious, got in, and drove off. We did all of that in twenty minutes. We had to get to my house and put the car in the garage. Lil was on lookout as we made the drive to my house. We both realized that it was very stupid to leave the gun in the woods because if Melvin caught up with us, we would have no defense.

CHAPTER 17

We made it to my house safely. Unbelievably, our phones still had power to them. The batteries had not died while they sat in my hot car for the last twenty-four hours. Our phones were ringing off the hook, but we decided to not answer them right away. We needed to wait until we processed what had just happened to us. Plus, we needed a story that would not trigger our husbands to fly back into town. They had left California two days ago to go to India to talk to one of the Investors who was on the verge of pulling out. I think the nine-hour time difference was helping us out.

Lil and I immediately went into the bathroom to shower and attempt to cleanse ourselves from the scum that was left within us. I actually felt like a garbage disposal, and I suddenly remembered what my mom use to tell me when I was growing up. She would say, "Don't let no man use you as a garbage disposal." What she was trying to tell me at that time was just don't give my goods up to anyone because all most men wanted at that age was to hit it and quit it. I felt just like a garbage disposal where those guys disposed of their waste inside of me. I grabbed my old fashioned hot water bottle, (Yes, the one that your grandma use to have hanging on the back of the bathroom door) filled it with water as hot as I could stand it, and put some white distilled vinegar in it. I ran myself a hot bath, but before I got in I looked under the cabinets in my bathroom to see if there was something I could use to remove any signs of those men from my body. I spotted the Clorox bleach. It was industrial strength, but at that point I could care less. I just felt dirty and disgusting and I needed to disinfect myself. I wondered if I could die from this however, it really didn't matter because I felt dead anyway.

I poured a capful of bleach into my bath water. Once I got into the tub, I sat down and didn't move for about ten minutes. I felt so numb. I kept having flashbacks of the rape, my ex-boss and his death, my children, and my husband. All I could think of was that I let my quest to be thin ruin my life. Looking at my current state, I really was not that bad. I had some extra pounds on me, but so what! I had a husband that loved me, and I had a beautiful family. The problem was that I didn't love myself. However, I promised myself that I was going to get some help immediately, and I was going to get my life back. I hoped Lil would go with me, because I couldn't live like that another day.

I stood up in the tub and inserted the tip of the water bottle into my vagina. It hurt me to do that, but I pushed through the pain. I squeezed the bottle so that the hot water and vinegar solution squirted into my vagina. Once I emptied the bottle, I sat back down in the water for another ten minutes. Then, I got out of the tub, dried myself off, and put on a sweat suit.

When I came out of my bedroom, Lil was already done with her bath and had escaped into the guest room. When I walked in, she was sitting on the floor with tears streaming down her face. I could tell that she had already smoked some of two eights that she conned the guy out of when we picked up my car. I went over to give her a hug, and we both stayed in that position for a while. I finally broke the silence and told her that we needed to get some help and that I was going to commit myself to a treatment facility. Lil did not respond. I pulled away from her and looked her in the face. She was emotionless and numb.

I slowly walked away, grabbed my pipe that was hidden in the nightstand drawer, put a piece of rock on it, and smoked it. It felt great. It took me away from the heaviness in my heart, the hurt, the shame, and the pain. I kept adding a rock onto the pipe, one after the other. I wanted it all to go away. When I looked over at Lil, she was still crying and surprisingly, she was not running from one room to the other closing doors like she normally did when smoking crack. That rape had taken so much from her. I don't know what Melvin did to her, but I did hear her screams. Neither of us were at a point where we can talk about it. It hurt too much. We made a huge mistake, and I really didn't know if it could be fixed. We knew that our husbands would find out. I just didn't want to be here when Ron did. Hopefully, I would be at the treatment facility.

We were down to the last rock, and Lil looked at me and said, "We have to find a way to get more."

"What? Lil, we can't go back out there! Do you understand what just happened to us? We were going to be killed, Lil. This is it, we have got to get us some help."

"I'm not going to no damn treatment facility. I will get me another eight. Don't worry about it."

"I can't believe you! After what we just went through, you are willing to risk your life again and go back out there?

"I don't give a shit, Sam! Let them kill me! I'm dead anyway! What, you think my husband is going to want to be with me now? I'm fucked up now, Sam. He's not going to want me."

"Lil, he doesn't have to know. I am not going to tell Ron about what happened to me. I agree that if he knew, I think it would change how he feels about me."

Lil was quiet for a few minutes before she agreed with me. She still said that she was not going to a treatment facility. I explained to her that if she stayed, Melvin would have his boys looking for us and they would kill us. I told her that we needed to get away to let the dust settle. She still said she was not going. I kindly said ok and told her that I was going to my bedroom to make a call to the Tranquil Gardens Treatment Facility that we saw advertised on TV. When I called Tranquil Gardens, I told them that I was going by the name of Mary Brown for now and that I would give them more information when I get there. They were located in Arizona. The travel time from Maryland to Arizona is approximately thirty-five hours driving. If we flew, it would take about three and a half hours. Of course, flying was better, but I didn't have access to a credit card with that type of money on it; plus, Ron would find out.

I pulled out my wallet so that I could check the balance on all of my credit cards. Sometimes, they would automatically increase my limit if my balance was close to the available credit. As I began checking the available balance on six of my credit cards, I saw the American Express card. The payment was due, but I was not in bad standing yet. My two Master cards were over the limit, my two Visa cards were over the limit, and my Discover had actually increased my limit by $10,000. I also saw the company Visa that Daniel gave me to use for supplies and anything the office needed. I wondered if the card was deactivated, so I called the 800 number, and my account was still active. There was no limit on the card because it was a corporate card. Daniel did not put a limit on it since it was for him. Immediately, my wheels began to turn.

I called the airlines and booked a first class flight to Arizona for both Lil and me. I used the corporate card that Daniel had given me. I decided that this corporate card would fund the entire trip and our stay at the treatment facility. I would deal with the consequences later. We were booked to fly out of BWI airport at 7:30a.m. the next morning. I went back into the guest room where Lil was seated on the floor with tears still streaming down her face. I sat down next to her, grabbed her hands, and told her that we were booked to fly out tomorrow morning. She still said she was not going. I told her she did not have much of a choice if she wanted to live. She just got quiet.

A few minutes later, she asked me how did I pay for the flights. I put a smirk on my face, and she asked me what was I up to. I told her that the corporate card for the company that we were no longer employed at was still active. I told her that our entire trip was going to be charged on that card. That seemed to bring Lil some joy. I think it felt good to hurt somebody like we had been hurt. Just like that, she said she would be ready to go. I'm not sure if she really meant it, but at least she was going. When I told her that we were flying first class, she gave me a huge smile. That was the first time I have seen her smile like that in a long time. I really miss how we used to be. We will never be the same again. We were ruined. We were numb. We were bitter. We were hurt. *God, please help us get out of this!*
As we got up to head downstairs, we heard a car pull up. We had been peeking out the windows all night and early this morning to make sure no suspicious vehicles rode by or parked on the street. A car pulled right into my driveway. Lil and I were nervous. When the young lady got out of the car, Lil and I both breathed a sigh of relief. It was Logan. I opened the door for Logan when she rang the doorbell.

She looked like she had not had any sleep in days, and she was scared. She explained to us that the police had taken her in for questioning. She said that a car had been following her, so she snuck away to her mom's house and got her mom's car. Lil and I looked at each other. Then, I jumped up and told Logan to move her car into my garage. I opened the garage so that she could pull in right next to my car. I looked around to see if anyone was looking.

Once Logan was in the garage, I pressed the garage door opener to close the door. She came in through the laundry room and sat down to explain everything. She said that she stuck to the alibi and said that we were at my house for a girls' movie night. I'm glad she told me what she told the police so that our stories could be straight. I know we discussed it, but I had forgotten parts of the story. Logan also said that someone else from work knew that she and Daniel was having an affair. She also explained to us that the same person also heard the argument between me and Daniel. She said that the person heard how Daniel berated me and also that he called Logan a slave. She said that the police were asking her if she knew where I was because they stopped by my house a few times and did not get an answer.

I knew that the person Logan was talking about was Sarah. Sarah always tried hard to get Daniel's attention, but he knew she liked him so, it was not a challenge for him. Plus, at that time, I really thought he was a good guy and was faithful to his wife. He didn't appear to like bleach blonds anyway. What little did I know.

When Sarah saw that Logan was getting more of Daniel's attention, she despised Logan. While Logan was telling us the story, the doorbell rang. I peeped out the window in the family room and saw a police car in front of my house. I told Logan to go upstairs and not to make a sound so that the police wouldn't know that she was there.

I opened the door for the police and there were two of them - one male and one female.

They asked if they could come in. I opened the door wider for them to enter and guided them to the family room where Lil was still seated. Once they sat down, the female officer asked if there was any reason why a black SUV with three guys in it was sitting in front of my house. I told her that I had no idea. She explained that when they pulled up, the guys drove off. The male officer chimed in and said that he put on his siren and pulled them over. He asked them what they were doing in a neighborhood like this. The driver said that he has a sister that lives out here and that he had not talked to her in years but wanted to break the ice. The police asked his sister's name and he gave him a name that actually registered. The cop told him where the house was, and they pulled off. Lil and I glanced at each other. Fortunately, the cops did not ask any more questions about the black SUV.

The male cop began to ask me about my relationship with Daniel. He asked me to tell him about the argument we had. I asked him what argument was he referring to. He said that one of the team members at my job said they heard Daniel and me arguing. I lied and told him that Daniel and I always have disagreements and that was the gist of our relationships. I went on to explain that since I manage his calendar, he wanted me to schedule some meetings when there was simply no room on the calendar. I informed him that he would need to cancel one meeting to replace it with the one he was requesting, but he did not want to do that. He wanted me to squeeze it in, but I refused. I explained to both cops that those were the only types of disagreements that Daniel and I had.

Then, the female cop asked me where I was on the day Daniel disappeared. I told her that we had a girls' movie night at my house. She asked who was in attendance at the movie night. I told her that it was me, Lil, and a co- worker named Logan. She wanted to know more about Logan. All I provided was that she was an assistant for the company, and she would cover for me when I went to lunch and when I had other meetings. For some reason, they never asked me about being fired. I wonder why no one said anything. Since most of the administrative staff was black, they must have heard what Daniel said about treating black women like slaves, and they were not going to say a word. Even the security guard was black. I went on to explain to the cops that our husbands were out of town and our children were away for the summer, so we would take turns staying the night at each other's houses.

They seemed pretty satisfied with the answers I gave them, and they both got up to leave. They handed me their business cards and told me that if I could think of anything that would help in Daniel's disappearance to give them a call.

After the cops left, Lil and I began to discuss the black SUV that the police saw in front of the house. We came to the conclusion that it was Melvin and his boys. They were coming back for revenge for what we did to them. I knew we should have killed them. We knew that since Melvin and his boys saw the police at my house, they would think that we turned them in. That was a good and bad thing. It's a good thing because they may not come to my house again for fear that the police were watching the house. The bad thing is that they would definitely be following us. Lil and I knew we had to leave for the airport immediately. Lil looked so scared. For the first time, I saw in her eyes that she was really ready to get some help. I yelled up for Logan to come downstairs. We had to tell her the entire truth.

"Logan, we need your help. We are in some trouble."

"What trouble are you in? How can I help?"

"We need you to take us to the airport.

Now!"

"Sure. I will take you to the airport. What is going on, Samantha?"

I explained to Logan about the experiment that Lil and I did, and she looked so shocked.

"Why would you want to try crack to lose weight? I think you look awesome. You get a lot of attention from the guys. I always wanted a shape like yours."

I was shocked to hear that because Logan was actually the size that I had been trying to get to all of my life. To hear her say that she wanted to be like me, totally shocked me. I went on to explain how both Lil and I got addicted to the crack and started visiting crack houses and got caught up with a drug dealer. I told her how he kidnapped us and was trying to kill us. I also explained that we were headed to Arizona to a treatment facility to get some help. I gave her the numbers for Ron, Michael, and my mother. I also gave her the number to the treatment facility. I told her to stop by to visit Ron after we had been in the facility for one week and give him the number and location. I instructed her to not tell him what happened to us and that I would tell him when he contacted me at the facility. Logan agreed, and Lil and I went upstairs to pack. We were not taking much. I mainly packed casual clothing and my personal hygiene products.

Logan drove us to the airport in her mother's car. During the ride, Lil and I were constantly looking at the cars that were next to us, behind us, and in front of us to make sure we were not being followed. The airport is about twenty minutes from my house, but the ride seemed especially long. Our flight did not leave until the next morning, but we felt that we would be safer at the airport than staying at one of our houses until the morning. It was exactly 4:00 p.m. when Logan pulled up in front of the airport. Lil and I got out of the car and grabbed our bags from the trunk. Logan got out to bid us farewell. We both gave her the last set of instructions. We insisted that she not contact our husbands until one week. That would be next Tuesday. I told her to call my cell if she needed anything or had any questions. I told her that we were going to send our husbands a text to tell them that we were going on a mini vacation. We would keep up the façade until she contacted them with the information on where we were. We hugged Logan tightly and thanked her again for all her help and support. She said she would keep us updated on any news with Daniel, and then we were off to our gate for our life saving journey.

Once we got through security, we found the sky club for the airline. Because our husbands travel so frequently, we were able to get a membership there. Once we entered the Sky club, Lil and I found a seat near the window in the back of the room. There were lounge chairs and sofas located throughout the club. It was perfect for times when travelers had long stays at the airport due to a cancelled flight - or in our case, arriving a day early for a flight departure. Lil and I ordered a drink. I ordered a martini with a double shot, and Lil ordered some Tennessee whiskey. I pulled my cell phone from my purse and began my text to Ron.

"Hi Baby! Hope everything is going well. It's been very hectic, but I will fill you in later. I wanted to let you know that Lil and I have an opportunity to go on a mini vacation to Arizona. She got a promotional deal for very cheap and asked me to go. I agreed. I hope you don't mind. We leave tomorrow. I will be back at the same time you get back from India. I miss you so much. I love you."

I hit send, turned my phone off, and ordered another drink. I showed Lil the text message I sent Ron so that hers could match up. Lil pulled out her phone and typed a text message to Michael. We had been dreading sending those text messages all day. Lil hit send on the text message to Michael and also turned her phone off. She ordered another drink, but this time, she asked for a Long Island iced tea. We gulped our drinks down and ordered a third round. I stuck with the martinis, and Lil stayed with the Long Island iced tea. No matter how much we ordered to drink, we could not get rid of the pain we both felt. We would hug and soothe each other to prevent ourselves from having a major breakdown inside the sky club in front of the folks in the club. Then, we continued drinking.

When the bartender started giving us dirty looks, we decided to make our eighth round our last. They were very strict in the sky club. If they thought that we were intoxicated, they may not let us on the flight. So, Lil and I moved to two of the reclining chairs and laid back. We didn't have much to talk about, which is really weird because we always had things to talk about. We would usually run out of time before we would run out of things to talk about. However, we were in a bad way, and we needed rescuing. I laid my recliner back, closed my eyes, and reflected on the last month. After about twenty minutes, I opened my eyes and Lil was knocked out. She was sleeping so peacefully. If only people knew what 'she had been through. I closed my eyes again, and I felt myself drifting slowly off to sleep, too.

When I woke up, only Lil and I were left in the club. I looked at my watch, and it was 5:30 a.m. I woke Lil and told her that it was time for us to go. I checked my phone to see if Ron responded, and he did.

"Hey Honey! I miss you deeply. How is my sweet baby? So, you want to get away without me huh? I think it is good for you. As long as you are home when I get home, I'm ok with it. I miss your good loving. Text me to let me know you made it to Arizona safely. Love you."

It was going to hurt Ron so much when he found out what I'd done. *I'm heading to get help baby, I hope you please forgive me,* I thought to myself. I put my phone back away, grabbed my bag, and we headed to our gate to board our plane to Arizona. The flight in first class was very nice and peaceful. I had another drink, and that put me to sleep. Lil also had another drink, and she went to sleep as well. I dreamed that my life was back to normal and none of this stuff happened to me - no rape, no addiction to crack, no job loss, and most of all no loss of self- respect. However, when I woke to the plane making a landing, reality hit me real hard. My life was truly in shambles.

CHAPTER 18

When we got off the plane and headed towards the baggage claim area, we looked around in disbelief. The treatment facility had a van to come pick us up. They would be waiting in the baggage claim area. The weather was hot, but it did not feel stuffy and make it hard to breathe like the DC weather. Although it was hot, the humidity was not stifling, and it felt comfortable to be out in the air. We spotted the driver with a sign that read: *Tranquil Gardens Treatment Facility*. It was rather embarrassing to have our business broadcasted out in public for all to see. I looked around to see if anyone was paying attention to the man holding the sign.

They were not so, I approached the driver and told him the fake name I gave over the phone. He looked at the list and confirmed my name as well as the name I gave for Lil and told us to follow him. It took about forty-five minutes for us to arrive at the treatment facility. There were two other people already in the van when we got in. They were both women who looked to be in their early thirties. As I gave them a once over, I wondered what their drug of choice was.

No one talked much during the ride. I think we were all pretty nervous. One of the girls was biting her nails. The other was constantly shaking her legs like one does when they have to go to the bathroom really bad. I was biting on my bottom lip, and Lil was constantly tapping her fingers on her purse. The noise was annoying but no one had the nerve to tell her to stop - not even me. It was too tense in that van.

Once the van pulled up in front of The Tranquil Gardens

Treatment Facility, we all grabbed our belongings and exited the van. We were escorted to the main lobby area where there was a team of four drug counselors waiting for us - one for each of us on the van. Joy Brown was the person who was assigned to me. Her name was very fitting. She gave me a big smile and welcomed me to the facility. We went into her office, I gave her my correct name and she processed me in by asking me all types of personal questions about my drug addiction, lifestyle, and family. When I told her I decided to try crack for two months to lose weight, she began to laugh and said that was good one.

Then, she asked me for the real reason why I became addicted to drugs.

When she looked at my face and saw that I was not joking, she apologized. She went on to explain that she had never had a case where someone tried drugs for weight loss. She assured me that I would succeed at the treatment there. I felt horrible. I could tell by the way she changed her attitude that she was embarrassed. Our meeting became uncomfortable because it felt like she was trying too hard to make me feel comfortable to make up for laughing at me. I was ready to go home, but I was stuck there. After she finished registering me, she asked me to empty out all of my belongings from my purse onto the desk. I felt violated, but nowhere near how violated I felt about being raped. It was still hard to say those words.

The next part of the meeting with Joy involved a medical examination. I was given a complete physical to assess my wellness. Joy asked me to take a detox test to determine if I had recently used drugs or alcohol. If I test positive for drugs and alcohol, my first step in the treatment process would be detox. I told her that I had alcohol on the plane and that I had smoked cracked two days ago. She did the test anyway and determined that I needed detox. I was escorted to an on-site detoxification area.

There were five rooms total in this area. I would be given medicine to help with withdrawals and to clean my system for five days. After the five days I would be assigned my room.

I was guided back to the lobby, and then the group of us that were on the van were given a tour of the facility. The facility was nice. The name was very fitting. It felt like a tranquil garden. It had a main area for watching TV, a game room, a meditation room, a medical facility, a cafeteria, and a small gym. We were guided outside to the courtyard area. We took a tour of the grounds of the courtyard. It was pure tranquility. There were beautiful paths lined with all sorts of flowers. I knew the names of a few of the flowers, but there were so many. It was very picturesque. There was a section for smokers and non-smokers. There was also a walking path that led around the entire facility. Benches were placed throughout the path. I knew instantly that I would be spending most of my time there on that path, sitting on the benches looking at the beautiful flowers.

Once we returned back to the lobby, we were all escorted to the detoxification rooms by our assigned drug counselor. Apparently, everyone on the van tested positive for drugs or alcohol and had to go through detox before getting assigned to a room. The detox was brutal. I believe that I got sick from the medicine they gave me, not the withdrawals. I never noticed myself having withdrawals from crack.

Maybe it was because when I wanted to smoke crack, Lil and I would find a way to get it. Since I didn't have crack anymore, and I had to take that medicine to clean my body, I was feeling an overwhelming amount of sadness and a sense of loss. I was at an all-time low and had never been in that state before. I no longer wanted to recover. I didn't want to face my family once they find out what I'd done.

For the next four days of my detox, all I did was cry and wish I was dead. After detox was completed, it was time for us all to be assigned to our rooms. My room was ok; it was clean. I had a twin size bed, a desk, and a dresser. It was decorated in a tropical scene and painted in a bright blue color. I'm sure they picked the tropical scene and the bright blue color to keep one uplifted. However, in my case, it was not working. I still felt the same sadness that I had when I was in detox. My counselor entered my room with me, and then she carefully searched through every item I had in my bag. Once she was done with the search, she told me to put my items away and she would see me at the next meeting, which was in two hours.

There was a package on my bed that listed all of the mandatory meetings as well as my daily session with my assigned counselor. There was a bathroom, but I had to share it with the room that was next to mine. The only problem with that was in order to get to the bathroom, I had to step out of my room and go next door because there wasn't an entrance to the bathroom from inside my room. I unpacked my belongings and placed them inside the dresser drawers. I heard the person in the room next to me unpacking. I was hoping it was Lil. I picked up my cell phone to call her when there was a knock on my door. When I opened it, Lil was smiling.

"Hey neighbor," she said.

I gave her a big hug. We were neighbors! I didn't have to share the bathroom with a stranger. She came into my room and we talked about how our family was going to react when they find out where we were and what we did.

We talked until it was time for the first meeting. It consisted of staff introductions and the introduction of all the patients of the treatment facility. The facilitator asked each staff member to introduce themselves. After the staff completed their introductions, the facilitator asked the patients that had been at the facility the longest to introduce themselves. Their introductions were honest and harsh. One woman talked about her addiction to heroin and how it ruined her life. She was a corporate lawyer and lost everything, including her husband and kids.

After hearing the stories of the others, I began to feel that there was hope because although the corporate lawyer lost everything, she said her husband and kids are working with her to get her well and bring her back home. She had a good support system. I prayed that Ron would forgive me and support me through this. I know Lil was thinking the same thing. With our husbands, we just couldn't be so sure. After the first meeting finished, we had personal sessions with our counselors that lasted most of the day. Once we were done, we ate dinner and had free time until the next day when it would start all over again.

After dinner Lil and I went directly to the courtyard and called Logan. She told us there was no update on Daniel and that she would be going to my house on Saturday to inform Ron of where we were. I explained to Logan that our husbands thought that we were at a conference with the company. I also explained to her that she should only tell them where we were and that we would explain the rest. She was clear on the instructions, and we really didn't have much else to discuss. I can tell she sensed the nervousness in me so she asked me to close my eyes, and she said a prayer for Lil and me. I had the call on speaker phone so Lil could hear her. During the prayer, I had tears running down my face. It felt good to have someone who was really concerned for our well-being instead of feeling judged for making a stupid decision. When the prayer was over, we ended the call. When I looked over at Lil, she had tears in her eyes as well. I hugged her and whispered in her ear that it felt good not to be judged. She nodded her head and began to cry uncontrollably. We walked the path along the courtyard and talked about our children. We knew that we had to get ourselves together for them.

We called my mother so that we could talk to our children. My mother said that they were at the pool. She asked how I was doing and that she had called a couple of times and didn't get an answer. I told her that I was in Arizona and had been back and forth at Lil's since Ron and Michael were out of town. She accepted that answer and did not ask any more questions, which meant that she believed me. She said that Ron had talked to the kids last week when he was at the airport headed to India. I asked how the kids were doing. The phone was on speaker so Lil heard the entire conversation. I asked my mother if Michael Jr. and Michele were doing ok. She said that they were having a ball. She complimented Lil on how well-mannered they were. She said that she taught Ronda and Michele how to make homemade biscuits. She also said that tomorrow they were learning to make homemade cookies.

Lil and I laughed and joked with my mother that they would need to put them on a diet when they get home. My mother said they had actually lost weight because they are very active at the day camp. After we hung up from speaking with my mother, Lil and I breathed a sigh of relief. We did not want our daughters to go through the same weight issues that we went through at that age. If only we had someone to tell us that we were good enough and someone to show us how to love our bodies. We went back to our rooms and Lil followed me into my room. I was glad because I did not want to be alone. I don't think she wanted to be alone either. We talked about our discussions with our husbands when they arrived. We promised again that we would not mention the rape.

It was getting late, and Lil finally went to her room. When she left, I took a shower, put on my PJs and got in the bed. Unfortunately, I could not go to sleep. I was awake and thinking of my life. My mind went over all aspects of my life. I was afraid, alone, and depressed. This reminded me of the feelings I felt when I was picked on at school about my weight. I thought about how I would go sit under the tree with Lil because no one wanted us to play with them because they said we were fat.

I knew that I was to blame for my current situation. I just wish I had someone in my life at that time to tell me that I was good enough, extra pounds and all. I didn't realize it then, but I now realize that when you are bullied in school, you internalize it and you carry that baggage with you for the rest of your life - unless you get help. I was raised that black people didn't get help. Therefore, any issues I faced was a private matter in my household only. We were threatened that if we mentioned anything that happened in our house to anyone, there would be hell to pay. So, I grew up dealing with things on my own, or so I thought. However, I wasn't really dealing with them. I was suppressing them. Now I'm here, smaller, but my life is fucked up. Yes, fucked up. I have to say it so harshly because that is my harsh reality. How will I get out of this?

CHAPTER 19

It had been exactly a week since Lil and I had been at the treatment facility. I talked to Logan this morning, and she was going to visit Ron at 11:00 a.m. eastern standard time. I knew he would often get up early, but that would allow time for him to sleep and account for the time change in India. I spoke with Ron when he got home. He asked how the conference was and I said it was great. I told him I missed him and that I had to go because the meeting was starting back up. Shortly after I ended the call with him, I got a text from him. He asked me if I was ok because I didn't sound like it on the phone. I didn't respond. I just couldn't lie anymore. Funny, I had been lying for the last two and half months, but I could not bear to tell him another lie. I just couldn't do it anymore.

It was going to be a whirlwind of activity once Ron finds out about where we were. I told Logan not to tell him anything else. I explained that he would pressure her, but I told her to say that was all she knew and that was the only instruction she got from me. I prayed that she stuck to the plan. Ron could be very persuasive and charming. Logan assured me that she understood, and she kept asking if I was ok. I told her that I was hanging in there. She was acting weird like she knew more than what Lil and I had told her. However, I knew she didn't because Lil and I promised that we would not tell anyone about our rape. It was very embarrassing. I thought that maybe I was overreacting and thanked Logan for all her help. She wanted to pray again with me before I ended the call. I closed my eyes and let her pray. This time her prayer was very powerful:

"Dear Heavenly Father:

You are an awesome God. Father God, you are our healer in all forms of sickness and pain. Your mercy endureth forever. I come to you today to ask that you place your blessings upon my friends Samantha Love and Lily Robinson. I ask that you look inside each of them Father God and remove anything which is unpleasing to your sight. I ask that you heal them from inside out God. Place your arms around them and fill them with your grace and mercy. Let them know that with you, all things are possible. Let them know that they can lean on you always and forever.

Touch them Oh Lord! Right Now God! Heal them! They are going through some major turmoil in their lives right now, and they need you now God. Please have mercy upon them. I ask that you bless their husbands God and guide them as they receive this information that I will provide to them today. Help them have empathy God and not anger. I ask that you bless the families that will be impacted by this God. Thank you for hearing my plea God and I ask all of this in Jesus' holy name. Amen."

Again, I was in tears after Logan finished her prayer. She had such a powerful prayer and the sincerity that she poured out grabs one's attention every time. I definitely needed God right now, and I hope that He would have mercy on me for all of the things I have done.

On Saturdays and Sundays, we don't meet with our therapist or counselors, but we have to attend the group sessions. The weekend is usually reserved for family and friends to visit.

The visiting hours are from twelve to five. I knew that my family would not be there, so I planned to spend the remainder of my day out in the courtyard. The weather was really nice. It was around 75 degrees, much cooler than the norm of 102 degrees that we had been experiencing since we had been at the treatment facility. Lil and I grabbed our phones and headed out to the courtyard. On the way out, we noticed how the lobby was full with family and friends waiting to see their loved one at the treatment facility. It made us very sad as we thought about our family and the hurt that we would cause them once they find out what we'd done. We knew that within a few minutes, our phones would start ringing.

As we strolled along the courtyard, we both had a nervousness that we just could not shake. We kept looking at our phones expecting them to ring. After about two hours of walking the courtyard, we became very suspicious because neither Lil nor I had received a call from our husbands. We decided to call Logan to see how the conversation with Ron went. Logan answered her phone on the first ring. I asked her how the discussion with Ron went. She began to apologize and explained that Ron forced her to tell him what happened. I asked her what she meant. She said Ron told her that she needed to give him information about me immediately, or he was calling the cops. She did not have a choice because she did not want the cops to come back to my place. Furthermore, she did not want them to see her there or they would try to make a connection about the murder. She kept apologizing. I told her that it was ok and asked her to give me blow by blow of the conversation with Ron.

Logan said that when she arrived at my house, she told him that she was a co-worker of mine and that she had some information that I wanted her to tell him. She said he was very hesitant, but he let her in and told her to have a seat at the kitchen table. Logan explained that once she was seated at the kitchen table, Ron sat across from her and asked her what was going on. She explained that we were in a treatment facility in Arizona and that we had been through some tragic situations. Logan said Ron did not believe her. She said he actually started laughing. He then asked her what tragic situations I was referring to. Logan said that is when she gave him the number to the treatment facility. She said Ron began to laugh and then told her that she was not going to come up in his house and tell him that his wife was at a treatment facility and give him a number to call. She told him that was all she had to tell him, just as instructed. However, Ron was not having it. She said he threatened to call the police, so she had to tell him about us being raped.

"What! How did you know that happened to us?"

"My brother told me about it. He runs in that circle."

"Oh My God! What else did Ron ask for?" "He asked for my brother's name, address, and number."

"Did he say why he wanted it?" I asked. "No."

"I'm scared, Logan. Ron has not called me at all. He must be furious with me. I did not want him to find out about the rape. What did your brother say?"

"He said that a few of the guys were bragging about gang banging two stuck up ladies from the upper class. I knew it was you and Lil. I asked him if they said what their names were. He said they kept referring to one of them named Lil as Melvin's girl, and that Melvin was looking for both of them to knock them off.

That's when I was sure it was you."

"They didn't tell him that we got away and could have killed them, but we didn't want a murder charge! Now they are bragging about it!"

"Did they really gang rape you two?" "Yes. I will tell you the story later. Right now, I need to know why Ron has not called me. Can you call your brother and find out?"

"He does not know that I know you and Lil. I didn't tell him that I knew Lil when he mentioned it. If I call him questioning him about it, he will know for sure that I know something."

I looked at Lil who was listening to the conversation the whole time. She had a looked of despair on her face which made me feel helpless, scared, and miserable. To top it off, our husbands knew where we were, and they had not contacted us at all.

***

After a long, sleepless night, Lil and I got up around eight o'clock to head down to get breakfast. Our husbands never called. That put us on edge, so Lil stayed in my room, and we stayed up all night trying to figure out what we were going to tell our husbands. We did not plan to tell them anything about the rape, but now that they knew, we were not sure how they were going to respond to us. Would they still want us? Would they lose respect for us? These were the types of questions that kept us up all night. We were both devastated. We were always worried about hurting our husbands. At this point, we were scared of our husbands. Scared of their reaction. Scared of what they would think of us. We had both been very strong, professional, independent women, and now we felt weak and dumb for smoking crack. We had let ourselves succumb to a damn substance that knocked us down to the lowest point of our lives.

As we were heading to the cafeteria, we heard a loud commotion in the lobby area. We heard one of the front desk clerks say, "Sir, I'm sorry, you can't come in yet, visiting hours are at twelve o'clock, and it is only eight."

When I heard the voice say, "I don't give a damn about the time, I want to see my wife right this second," I knew it was Ron.

I then heard Michael chime in, "I need to see Lilian Robinson right now, and there is nothing you can say that will stop me."

They were so angry and irate. Lil and I paused in our tracks, looked at each other, and turned around to go back to our rooms to hide. As we started to walk back, both Ron and Michael's voices began to get louder and louder. Lil and I stopped, and I said that we would have to face it head on, right then. Lil disagreed. She did not want to go face Michael. I pulled her and dragged her until we were in the lobby where we could be seen. She straightened up, and we both walked toward the lobby where our husbands were acting out. When Ron and Michael saw us approaching, there was immediate silence. I felt like we were in a twilight zone. They seemed shocked to see us. They looked at us as if they didn't know us. When we reached the point where we were standing in front of them, I gave Ron a hug, and he barely hugged me. His jaw was twitching, as he tried to contain his anger.

Michael did not hug Lil. Instead, he began shouting at her.

"What the fuck have you done, Lil?"

That is when the front desk attendant asked Michael and Ron to leave and come back at noon. Michael told her that he was not going anywhere and that he needed a private place to talk to his wife. She finally got the point that she was going to lose this battle. She then told Lil and me that they could go to our rooms. She also informed us of the policy that they do not hold a patient at their will and that we could leave if we wanted to go. She was fed up with us, and it felt like she just wanted us out of there. Ron said that they would get a hotel room at the Marriott down the street and he instructed us to come with them. We obeyed. His voice was firm and demanding, and that was not the time to disagree. Lil and I followed our husbands out of the facility and got into the rental car they had. They must have taken a flight out right after Logan talked with Ron, which explained why we had not heard from them.

During the drive to the hotel, Ron was quiet as he drove. Michael was on the phone making reservations at the Marriott, and Lil and I were quiet in the back. We both had tears rolling down our faces. I saw Ron glance at me from the rear view mirror a few times. The look in his eyes showed anger and disappointment. That was no way near what I was feeling. I know I hurt him deeply, and I didn't know if our marriage would recover from this. He pulled up to the hotel, valet parked, opened the door for me, and placed his hand on the lower part of my back to guide me into the hotel lobby. I did not know if that was for show to make everyone think that everything was fine, or whether he really still loved me and wanted to do that because I was his lady and he was proud to show it. Michael opened the door for Lil, and once she got out, he walked into the lobby with Lil trailing behind him.

While Michael and Ron were at the registration desk checking in, Lil and I went over to the lobby area and sat on the sofa in front of the fireplace. We looked at each other, but neither of us said a word. We were afraid to speak. After Ron finished, he walked over to me and said, "Let's go." His voice was firm and matter of fact. Lil and Michael trailed behind us. Our rooms were on the fifth floor. We were the only ones on the elevator headed up to our room. No one said a word. Ron just stared at me. Michael looked down as if he saw something on the floor. Never in my life, since knowing Ron, had we been silent on an elevator with Lil and Michael. We were always cracking jokes or laughing, but this silent treatment was brutal.

My heart was beating so fast that I could feel it beating through my chest. That was the day where it is determined whether I would get better or worse. It all depended on what my husband said and how he responded. We all got off the elevator and headed towards our rooms. Ron and I went to the left once we got off of the elevator, and Lil and Michael went to the right. I believe they did that intentionally for privacy. It took so much for me to make it those few steps from the elevator to our room, but I made it.

Once we got in the room, I went and sat on the sofa. Ron lost it then.

"What the fuck is going on Sam? I leave town and when I come back, I have some fucking stranger knocking on my mother fucking door telling me that you are in a treatment facility. Do you know what I did when she told me that? Huh? I laughed at that bitch because I know my wife would never touch anything illegal. Then, I fucking call the treatment facility and they tell me that you are a patient there!

Can you fucking believe that? I sure the fuck couldn't! Now tell me, how is it that my wife has been betraying me all of this time and I had no idea. Huh?"

I tried to answer, but Ron just kept going on and on.

"Do you know how embarrassing it is to have to be told that your wife is in a treatment facility? Do you give a fuck about your kids?

Huh? Answer me!"

I started to talk, and he cut me off again. "And, you know what that bitch told me?

She told me you and Lil were raped! How can someone rape my wife, Sam?"

He picked up the lamp and through it on the floor. I was crying. Ron was so mad. He was really hurt.

"You see what doing drugs can lead to now don't you? Someone took my precious goods and damaged them. How the fuck could you let this happen Sam? How?"

Suddenly there was a knock at the door. Ron went to answer it. It was the hotel security. He said he got a complaint about screaming in the room. Ron told him that we were having an argument and that we would try to keep it down. After hotel security left, Ron went over to the bar and grabbed him some rum and drank it down instantly. He took another bottle of rum and downed that, too. Then, he sat on the bed and just stared at me for about twenty minutes.

I knew I had better not leave out one detail. I got up to get a drink from the bar, but then I realized that I am trying to get sober. Therefore, I turned around and sat on the bed next to Ron and told him the story of how I planned to try crack for two months to lose weight and then quit. When I told Ron that Lil and I decided to try crack for two months to lose weight, he lost his mind.

"Is that how all of this started? So you can lose weight, Sam? How many fucking times have I told you that I love you as you are? Do you know how many skinny women try to get me to take them out? I'm in love with you just as you are. The funny thing is, you lost weight, but look at your life now, Sam. Is it worth it?"

I shook my head no. Ron asked me to continue with the story. I told him when Lil and I started smoking crack. I told him how we were getting the crack at first because of Lil and Melvin, but when she cut him off, he started acting crazy. I told him about the incident that happened when we visited the first crack house. I told him about Daniel and how Logan's brother killed him and disposed of his body so no one would ever find him. I revealed that Lil and I used to smoke on our lunch break and that we would go to hotels. I explained how we stopped that and started going to our houses when the kids left and when he and Michael were out of town. It took about one hour to give him every detail of everything that happened.

I even told him how I made a crack pipe and that before I had the pipe I used a soda can. He listened intently. All while he was listening, his jaw was twitching. He was still angry, but to me, it seemed like he softened up just a little bit. When I stopped talking and told him that was it, he looked at me and shook his head.

"No it isn't Sam. I want to know everything. You hear me? Everything! Who the fuck raped you? I want every detail of what happened."

I started crying hysterically.

"Ron, I really can't go over that again. Please don't make me do it. They hurt me so bad!"

"Tell me! Now!" he yelled.

I explained in detail how Melvin kidnapped Lil and me and forced us to his house. I continued to cry through my talking, and Ron had to tell me to pause, wipe my face, and talk so that he could understand me. I went on to explain that once we got to Melvin's, Lil was taken into one room and I was taken into another. I explained to him how I was raped by the three guys. I told him how they tied me up and had their way with me, and that they all used condoms, but I was violated. I told him how I screamed for help and begged them not rape me because I had children depending on me.

I was screaming at the top of my lungs. As I told the story of the rape to Ron, all of the emotions of pain and hurt came rushing through me. I felt as though I was experiencing it all over again. For the first time since Ron had been in my presence, he reached out to me and held me close. We both cried together. He held me so tightly that I felt comforted knowing that he still had feelings for me. When I tried to kiss him, he turned away from me. He explained that he did not know whether he could deal with this or if he would be able to be intimate with me anymore. He took one last dig at me, and it hurt me to my core.

Ron said to me, "You see, Sam. You lost the weight, but you could now lose your husband. Now you tell me, was it worth it?"

I could not believe he said that to me after I had just poured my heart out and explained to him what happened to me. I was devastated. I just stared at him. He got up and walk out of the room.

***

138

It had been an hour, and Ron was still gone. I heard a knock on my door and when I opened it, it was Lil. She ran into the room and told me that Michael is furious with her. I told her that Ron walked out on me, and I didn't know where he went. Lil informed me that Michael and Ron were outside in the car talking. Then, she asked me how it went with Ron. I told her that I told him everything. I explained that since he had already found out about the rape, I had nothing else to lose. She asked me if I told Ron about her and Melvin. I told her that he knew we were getting the crack from him until Melvin got mad when she stopped seeing him.

Lil screamed.

"You told him that I was sleeping with Melvin! How could you, Sam?"

"Lil, I was just being honest with Ron and putting everything on the table. I didn't want to leave anything out just in case he finds out from somebody. You know our husbands know the streets based on their upbringing, and they still have connections."

"I am so screwed right now. When I was explaining to him about us deciding to try crack to lose weight, he was so insulting. He called me an idiot and uneducated. He had such a look of distaste on his face when he looked at me.

Because of that, I could not bring myself to tell him about me sleeping with Melvin for crack," she cried.

"I know the feeling. Ron was just so angry. He was fuming. I thought I had a breakthrough with him when I told him about the rape. I was crying so hard that he hugged me and held me. When I tried to kiss him, that's when he turned away and walked out the room. But, here's the kicker, Lil…"

"What?"

"He got one last dig in and said to me, 'You see, Sam. You lost the weight, but you could now lose your husband. Now, you tell me, was it worth it.' And then, he got up and walked out."

"Damn, that was cold, Sam."

"Yes, it was, and he has not been back up here since. I don't think he is going to forgive me."

"I know once Michael finds out about Melvin, he will not forgive me either. I can honestly say that my marriage is over."

"You don't know that yet, Lil."

"Girl, you know damn well how Michael is. If it affects his ego, he's done. He would never find out his woman was unfaithful and stay with her.

He always felt like that and said it throughout our marriage."

"Things change, Lil. All we can do now is pray. Pray for our husbands and children. Our children's lives are going to be turned inside out."

"I know. It pains me to think of it."

Lil and I sat quietly on the sofa in the hotel room and let our minds drift off. My mind drifted off to what the scene would look like when Ron would tell the kids that I was at a treatment facility. If he was still harboring the anger that he has today, he would definitely make me look like a bad person to our children. Lil didn't make a sound. She continued to sit on the sofa and began to rock back and forth. We used to do that when we were young sitting under the tree when we were bullied. For some reason that rocking back and forth gave us comfort. I grabbed her hand, and we rocked back and forth together. We didn't make a sound, but I could feel some of the tension I had within my body began to release.

After about ten minutes of rocking, the door to the hotel room opened and in came Ron and Michael. I got up off the sofa where I was sitting with Lil to let Michael sit next to her, and I sat on the bed. Ron sat on the bed next to me with some distance between us. There was no sense of affection or comfort coming from him.

He didn't even want to look at me. Michael began the conversation.

"I asked Ron to let me come to this room so the four of us can get things out in the air. Apparently, there were some things that was left out in the conversation with Lil and me, and I want to discuss it with you here, Sam."

I said okay, and he looked directly at me.

Then, he asked me to explain how Lil was fucking Melvin. Before I could respond, Lil chimed in.

"Michael, I didn't tell you about that because you were being so mean to me. The things you were saying about me trying crack to lose weight were so harsh, that I did not want to endure the pain that you would cause if I told you about Melvin and how we got the crack from him."

"I deserved to know fucking everything!

Ron and I both do. You think I give a fuck about how it may hurt your feelings? How the fuck do you think we are feeling right now? Well, let me speak for myself... I know I'm fucked up about it, and I want to knock the fuck out of you. I can't stand to look at you right now."

Ron chimed in to give his peace.

"Oh most definitely. I'm fucked up over this, and the fact that the love of my life tried crack to lose weight, got raped, and then ended up in a treatment facility. I mean, am I dreaming, man? This shit is fucked up. This does not happen in real life. Everybody knows that crack is very addictive. Who the fuck would say they would try it for two months and then quit! I mean, all you had to do, Sam, was look at your sister Marie. She is still out there. Where was the common sense here? This shit is fucked up!"

"Ron, all I can say is that I'm sorry. I never meant to hurt you. Michael, I'm also sorry. Lil and I were just so desperate to be thin because we thought that would keep you guys interested in us. We were not thinking logically. Yes, it was a stupid, ignorant, dumb, unintelligent, and any other words you want to use, decision. We just weren't thinking because of the desire to be smaller. I hope one day you two can forgive us. I know that will not happen soon, but I made my bed so I have to lay in it."

"Well, we all know you have done enough
of that don't we?"

Michael was so rude. He did not have to say it like that. Lil jumped up and got right in his face.

"You think it is my fault that I got raped, Michael? How dare you! Yes, I made a mistake, and I am paying dearly for it. However, I will not sit here and listen to you tell me that getting raped - and I mean ganged raped - is my fault. You are a fucking asshole! How could I have married somebody who has no sympathy or let alone empathy for what has happened? I know you are mad, Michael, but give me a fucking break! It is not all about you!"

"You know what. I don't want to hear this shit. I'm outta here."

Michael left the room and we were left sitting there. Lil started talking with Ron. She always had a way of making him come around when he and I were in a disagreement.

"Ron, I know you are angry. Yes, we were stupid. Yes, we should have known better. Yes, we had so much to lose, and we're losing it. All I can say is that Sam and I have always struggled with our weight.

You know the stories of how we were picked on in grade school. Hell, that is how Sam and I became best friends. Ron, what you may not understand is that our weight has been the number one hindrance in our lives. We wake every morning thinking about it, and we go to bed at night thinking about it. You and Michael never knew the struggle that we faced, because we kept you out of it. However, Sam and I would talk all the time.

"At times, she would call me crying thinking that you were not happy with her anymore because of her weight. Oh, and when you have your office parties and Sam goes, the women would make fun of her. She never told you that, did she? Of course she didn't because she shielded you from a lot of stuff she dealt with. Granted all of this is due to low self- esteem. So again, yes it was very dumb and immature to try crack to lose weight. All I can say, and I know I speak for Sam when I say this, is that it was done out of desperation.

Desperation to be the eye candy on our husbands' arms when going to events. Desperation to look in the mirror and feel good about how we looked. Desperation to live life instead of hiding. There were many functions where we made excuses to not attend because we didn't want anyone to see us. We didn't want your peers to see that you had fat wives.

"Ron, this goes so deep. So please don't judge us. Just know that we never meant to hurt you, we really believed that we would try it for two months, lose the weight, and be done with it. We were so wrong, Ron. Please forgive us and don't hate us. Now, I'm going to find my husband to try to explain to him. I think I may need your help here. You know how Michael is."

"You stay here with Sam, and I will go and talk to Michael. For the record, I heard what you said and you helped me see things from a different perspective. Right now, I am hurting, but I will do my best to try to work through this. It's not going to be easy, and I can't promise you, Sam, that our relationship will be ok. I'm just not there yet."

Ron walked out the room to find Michael. I told Lil that she did a great job explaining to Ron how I felt and that she put in words that I would probably never would have found. Lil said that she believed that Ron will eventually come around, but she didn't think Michael would.

This ordeal can be very stressful on the body. I got up on the bed and laid down because I had a headache from all the crying and talking. Lil crawled up next to me, and we both fell asleep.

We woke up to the sound of Michael and Ron's voice along with the aroma of french fries and burgers. We were starving. Michael looked like he calmed down some. They gave us our bag with the burgers and fries in it along with a drink. Ron gave me a strawberry milkshake.

When he gave it to me, we made eye contact and he looked away really quick. I only ordered a strawberry milkshake when I had been really good with my weight and as a reward, I would get a shake. I felt so proud that he would get that for me. I think it was his way of saying he loved me, but he was not ready to tell me yet. That one gesture put me in a very good mood.

Michael got Lil a diet coke. That is what she always ordered. Lil knew that I only drank a milkshake on special occasions. She bent over and whispered in my ear, "I told you, he will come around."

CHAPTER 20

When we got back to the treatment facility, Ron and Michael did not go in. Ron told me that he needed time to think about everything and would call me when he was ready to discuss next steps. Lil said that Michael told her the same thing. We didn't ask any questions and accepted what they told us. Ron got out of the car, came around to my side, and opened the door. He gave me a quick hug and got back in the car. To my surprise, Michael got out of the car and opened the door for Lil. He gave her a tight hug and apologized for being rude to her.

He then said that he was not ready to forgive her. He would call her with his decision on how he is going to move on - whether it be with or without her. Lil did not say anything, and we both looked back and waved at them as we were walking inside the treatment facility.

When we arrived at the lobby, our assigned therapists were there waiting for us. The front desk associate must have called them to fill them in on what happened. We would have to go through the story and explain why our husbands acted out, and then they were going to make us take a test to make sure we were clean. We both passed the test. My counselor wanted me to explain how my husband was feeling about my drug abuse. I reminded her that I had not told him. I told her that he was upset when he found out from a friend. I explained to her that he booked a hotel room at the Marriott so that we could discuss my actions. She asked me how I felt. I was honestly able to tell her that I had a glimmer of hope.

She gave me tips on how to cope with stress and reminded me to ensure that I make every appointment because it was critical for my success. She grabbed my hand and apologized for thinking that I was joking when I told her I tried crack to lose weight. I told her that she did not have to apologize, because although it was not funny as I sat in front of her at the treatment facility, it is unheard of. She gave me a hug, and I was on my way to my room to rest. After a sleepless night and the emotional ride at the hotel with Ron, my body was worn out. I needed a good night's rest. Lil was leaving her therapist's office as I walked out of my therapist's office. We walked up to our rooms together. Lil was exhausted too, and she could barely hold her eyes open. She said that she was exhausted, emotionally and physically. We gave each other a hug, said good night, and then retreated to our rooms.

***

Two weeks passed, and I had not heard anything from Ron. I thought that he would need about a week to cool off and come around, but not two weeks and counting. I had not received a phone call, message, or text from him.

Lil had not heard anything from Michael either. It seemed like Ron and Michael were planning their moves as it related to Lil and me. I couldn't be upset about it because we are connected at the hip, and we do everything together. I got this bright idea to call Logan to see if Ron had contacted her anymore, but she was very tight lipped. She said that Ron had told her that he would call the police on her if she made contact with us again. How could he do that? Ron was being very cruel. Logan did not deserve that kind of treatment. She was so scared. Because I like her and didn't want her to face anymore triumph in her life, I decided not to pressure her.

For the life of me, I just could not understand Ron's actions and why I had not heard from him yet. I thought we had made some kind of headway when he gave me that strawberry milkshake. I guess it was all just deception. Shame on me for thinking he really cared. Lil and I continued with our treatments at the facility. We were working very hard. My goal was to walk out of this treatment facility in five weeks healthy, healed, and free of the need for crack cocaine or any drug. Although the routine at the facility was getting boring and I missed my kids like crazy, I had to stay focused for them. I didn't know what Ron told them, but for some reason, my cell phone no longer rang anymore with them wanting to talk to me. I also had not received a call from my mother. I was afraid to call her because I didn't know what she knew either. Therefore, I decided to wait.

My life was falling apart, so I waited. That reminded me of the poem I wrote years ago when I was tired of being tired:

I've been told that life is a wonderful thing, so I wait.
I have no reason for living, so I wait.
I have been told that there is joy in giving, so I wait.
Pain may come at night, but joy comes in the morning, so I wait.
At times I look in the mirror and hate what I see and ask God to please help me, so I wait.
Some people's blessings are overflowing, so I wait.
You reap what you sow, so I wait.
My pain is hard to bear but I'm told if I hang on, my life will be spared, so I wait.

I remember reciting that poem at a time in my life when nothing was going right. It's funny how I suddenly remembered it right at the point when I was going through some major struggles. It seemed pretty fitting to me, so I pulled a sheet of paper from my bag, wrote it down on the paper, and taped it to my wall. I would use it as a reminder of how I got through my struggles and had a wonderful life.

***

Today marked the third week that Lil and I had not heard from our husbands. I had no idea what was going on. I wanted to call Ron, but he told me that he would call when he was ready.

The weekend was approaching, and I swear that I couldn't bear to pretend that it was alright that I didn't have any family members coming to visit me. On the visiting days, Lil and I escaped to the courtyard and hung out there for hours. It was a really hot day, we stayed out there as long as we could stand it. It is supposed to be 105 degrees tomorrow. I knew Lil and I won't be out in the courtyard for long. We would mainly just hang out in our rooms.

Today was another usual day at the treatment facility. When I finished my meetings and met with my therapist, I went up to my room and went to bed. I had no desire to converse with the other patients. Lil was hanging out in the recreational area with a few of the other residents. I waved to her and signed that I was going to sleep by putting my two hands together and laying my head on them. I don't know if that is the official sign language symbol for sleep, but Lil knew what I was telling her. She blew me a kiss and signed back that she loved me by making a cross on her chest by taking her right hand and using her forefinger and drew a cross. Now that I think about it, that is the sign for God bless you not I love you. Oh well, which ever one it was, I accepted it by nodding at her, and then I went on my way.

When I woke up the next morning, I had a sense of clarity. I felt that God had visited me while I was sleeping. The message was that everything was going to be ok and that I had to keep moving as though I was in a state of despair. God told me that He would make it work, but I had to show anybody that may be watching me that no matter what is thrown at me I am a Christian. In other words, be joyful and thankful for waking up and continue to do His will every day, and live my life in a way that is pleasing to his sight at all times. So what I won't have any visitors today. I woke up today. That's a blessing. I have an opportunity to go to the courtyard to look at the beautiful flowers that he has blessed us with. I will no longer take things for granted, despite my situation. God has forgiven me. That was all I needed.

I called Lil and told her about my message from God. She listened to me and somehow, I inspired her. We agreed that going forward, we would have no more pity parties. We would praise God and thank Him each and every day. We would ask him to guide our steps and give our sorrows and worries to Him and forget it. We made our plans for the day and ended the call.

We were going to meet in the cafeteria at ten o'clock for breakfast and then head to the courtyard. If we got too hot, we were going to head to the theatre room and find a good movie to watch.

We ate breakfast and headed outside just around noon. Families had already started to arrive. Lil and I made it to the courtyard and went to our favorite spot where we sat at the bench and looked at the beautiful flowers. The colors seemed so vivid today. There was purple, blue, yellow, pink, lavender, and orange flowers.

They were landscaped in such classic way. The landscape designer had a sharp eye for contrast and detail. We continued to sit and admire those flowers and every so often, when a slight breeze would blow, the aroma from the flowers would fill the air, and if you closed your eyes, it made you reminisce about being in a field in the country filled with thousands of wildflowers. I had images of running through those fields without a care in the world. Then, there was a car horn that interrupted my thoughts and as I opened my eyes, I saw Ron and Michael in a silver SUV blowing the horn at me and Lil. I stood up and Michael put his head out of the window and said, "Don't you ladies go anywhere. We are going to park and will be right back."

When they pulled off, Lil and I began jumping up and down and hugging each other. Our husbands had come back! Lil asked me if I noticed how nice Michael sounded. I told her that I absolutely did and that I was actually surprised. We hugged each other again and then sat down. We didn't want to show too much excitement just in case they were bringing us bad news. Once they parked, Ron and Michael came over to the bench where Lil and I was sitting. Ron gave me a long affectionate hug. I could have cried right at that very moment, but I remembered my instructions from God last night. I hugged him tightly and told him that I was very glad to see him. Michael embraced Lil like he really missed her, too. I was so happy.

We sat down and talked about the treatment facility and gave them updates on our progress. Ron said that they have rooms at the Marriott again. He told us to go in and tell the team that we were staying with our husbands and would be back tomorrow. We signed out and got into the SUV and headed towards the hotel.

During the drive, we caught up on things that were going on in the neighborhood back at home. No one dared to bring up the elephant in the room. I'm sure in due time, it would be addressed. Once we got into our room, Ron poured himself a drink. He asked me to sit down on the bed. He told me that he made a decision on how he wanted to proceed. I was so nervous. I actually was shaking. I asked him to excuse me for a moment because I had to use the bathroom. I went into the bathroom, got on my knees, said my prayer to God and asked him to fix my situation.

I flushed the toilet and ran the water like I had used the bathroom. I went back out to the room with confidence and determination to face any decision Ron throws at me without falling to pieces. Once I sat back down on the bed, Ron grabbed my hand. *Good start*, is what I said to myself. He proceeded to tell me that although I hurt him very bad, he knew that I was hurting even worse. He said that he does love me and wants to try to make things work between us. He also said that he did not know how or if he would respond to me sexually again. However, one thing he did know was that it would take time for him to get over it. He said it was not my fault, but then he turned around and said that if I hadn't decided to try crack again, none of this would be happening.

"So, you are saying that it is my fault right, Ron?"

"Well Sam... I'm not here to hurt you or to argue, but let's call a spade a spade. If you didn't get yourself in that ridiculous situation, we wouldn't be having this conversation right now. Right?"

"You're right. I can't argue with you. Do you know how much I blamed myself? Do you know how I beat myself up every day? I can't apologize enough. I'm so sorry for the pain I caused you, Ron. Please know that. I'm truly sorry and I will do everything I can to fix this, if you allow me."

We continued our talk into the wee hours of the night. We ordered room service when we got hungry, ate our meal, and began talking some more. It was exhausting, but it needed to be done. Ron had time to think about everything that happened for three weeks. He was full of questions that he needed me to answer and he wanted every detail. When he felt that I was leaving out something, he would stop me and ask more detailed questions. I thought I was on trial. After I finished answering all of Ron questions about starting crack, how I smoked it, when I smoked, visiting the crack house, visiting Melvin's house, and the rape, it was about one o'clock in the morning.

Ron then began to ask me about Daniel and wanted to know every detail. He wanted to know about Logan. I told him about walking in on them and the argument Daniel and I had. I told him what he said about treating black women as slaves. Ron's jaw began to twitch again. He was pissed. He began asking more questions. I told him about Logan's brother and how he said he took care of Daniel and how he said that no one would ever find him. I told him how the police came to the house to question me about Daniel and how nobody at the job reported that I was fired. Lastly, I told him that I was using the corporate card to pay for me and Lil's stay at the treatment facility.

After I finished spilling my guts, Ron pulled me over to him and kissed me gently. He pulled me up to lay on top of him and held me tight. He whispered in my ear that he loved me. Then, he whispered that I would never have to worry about Melvin and the three guys that hurt me ever again. I raised up so that I was looking him directly in his eyes.

"What do you mean?"

"I mean, that they will never bother you again. You don't have to worry about them again."

"How do you know that they won't bother me Ron"

"Let's just say, I handled it."

"What do you mean? Handled what?" "All you need to know is that they are taken care of, and you don't have that worry hanging over your head. The less you know, the better. Now, don't ask me anything else about them motherfuckers or ever bring their names up again."

I laid my head on Ron's chest, and we fell asleep. It felt so good to have his body next to me. I missed him so much. I knew that if I tried to get him to make love to me, that it would be out of the question because he was not ready. However, I know that Ron loves a good blow job. I began kissing him on his neck and as I kissed him, I slowly unbuttoned his shirt. I moved slowly down to his nipples. His wife beater t- shirt was in the way so, I moved it to the side so that I could get to his left nipple. I licked and sucked his left and right nipple, rotating between the two, until they hardened up. I noticed that "Rocky" had also risen to attention. Ron was unable to tame his emotions - he was getting very aroused. He sat up and removed his shirt, t-shirt, and pants. He intentionally left his underwear on. I know that by leaving his boxer briefs on, he was telling me that he was not ready to enter me, but he was definitely on board for me going down on him.

As I approached Rocky, he was large and stiff just as I remembered. I wish I could put him up into my vaginal shaft and ride him like a wave at this moment but, I know it will take time. I massaged Rocky gently and began to stroke every single contour of his penis. I love it when I take my tongue and make swirling motions with it on the tip of the penis and around the edges. It gives me so much pleasure. Also, it makes Ron lose control, he was panting due to the pleasure. I put my warm moist lips over the entire shaft and worked my head up and down slowly, and then faster and then slow again. I rotated between fast, slow and deep throating Rocky until Ron could barely hold his composure. He loves it when I take as much of him as I could bear in my mouth and down my throat. Finally, Ron lost his composure and his future kids exploded all in my mouth and all over my face. I usually don't swallow but, today, I wanted my man back so, whatever it takes, I'm down. I got up and wiped my face and brushed my teeth and went back to lay in my man's arms. It was a good day.

We were awakened by the sound of taps on our door. We both jumped up and put on some clothes. When Ron opened the door, it was Lil and Michael. They looked happy. Lil must have orally entertained him just as I did Ron. I knew Lil would give me the scoop when we got back to our rooms. Lil and Michael stopped by to see if we wanted to have breakfast with them at the restaurant on site at the hotel. Their food is pretty good. We told them to give us twenty minutes and we would be down. We told them that we would also check out since it was close to check-out time.

During breakfast, we talked about the remaining weeks we had left at the treatment facility and talked about our kids coming home from my mother's place. Although Lil and I had not had a chance to talk, it was clear that she and Michael had made some progress. Then Michael dropped a bomb shell at the table. He said, looking directly at Lil and I, that he had been thinking and although he had not had a chance to discuss with Ron, he would feel much better if we got an AIDS test. I immediately looked at Ron. He did not know how to respond. I asked if he felt the same way. He said that he had not thought about it but to be safe, he thinks that it's a good idea. I explained to them that the guys that raped me used condoms. I also told them that I could not believe we were having this conversation in a restaurant.

However, if it would make him feel better, I would get tested. I looked at Lil and she said that she had no problem at all taking the test. I knew Lil wanted to take the test because she and Melvin had sex without a condom at least one time. We agreed to take the test when we got home.

As we finished our breakfast, Ron and Michael got up to walk out front to pull up the car. Lil and I were glad they left, because we had a chance to do a quick catch up on the activities last night.

"So, did you and Michael make love? He is sure in a good mood, Lil?

"We didn't have sex, but I gave him a good blow job and he was happy."

"I did the same for Ron. Although I wanted to make love, he was not ready. Now Michael brings up this AIDS shit right when things were going well. He sure knows how to kill the mood."

"That's Michael for you, the biggest ass out of the bunch!" Lil said.

"Did Michael say anything to you about the guys that raped us?"

"No. What do you mean?"

"Ron said they would never bother me again. When I asked him what he meant, he said that they were taken care of and to never bring their names up again."

"Oh my God, Sam! What do you think they've done? We need to find out. Let's call Logan when we get back to the room."

"Logan is not going to talk. Ron scared the hell out of her."

"We will get her to talk. Just follow my lead."

During the ride back to the treatment facility, Ron and Michael were pretty quiet. Once we pulled up to the facility, Ron and Michael both got out to open the doors for us. As we were walking in, Ron told me that it was great spending time together and although we weren't nowhere near being back where we used to be, it was a start. He kissed me on my lips and said that he would call me when he got to the airport. Their flight was scheduled to leave in three hours so he and Michael were heading to the airport. He said that the next time he would see me would be to pick me up and take me home.

Michael and Lil said their goodbyes, and Michael kissed Lil very passionately and told her that he would talk to her later.

When we got upstairs to our rooms, Lil came into my room with me. She wanted to call Logan to see if we could get any information out of her about the guys that raped us. We wanted to know if anything happened to them. I called Logan and when she answered she immediately informed me that she can't talk to me. She said she did not want to get in trouble with Ron and have him call the police on her. Even though she did not do anything, she knew things that could incriminate her brother and she didn't need the police hounding her. She said because of that, and the things that has happened with Daniel, Ron, and me and Lil, she was moving out of state. I asked her where she was moving but she declined to tell me because she wanted to keep her distance and have peace. Since I had Logan on speaker phone, Lil heard the entire conversation and chimed in. She told Logan that we needed one more favor before she left town.

Logan instantly declined before Lil had the chance to tell her what the favor was. Lil told Logan that although Ron threatened her about calling the police, she could also call them and that she knows a lot more than Ron. Logan lost it.

"What! I can't believe that you are blackmailing me! After all I have done for you both!"

I chimed in because I did think Lil was being a little harsh with Logan.

"Logan, I don't think Lil meant what she said. She is just desperate, just as I am, but we don't mean to bring you any harm. All we need is some information from you, and then you can leave town and never have to speak to us again. Although I'm not comfortable with that, I would love to at least chat by email."

"I can drop you a line or two by email, Sam. That is not a problem."

"Great."

"What kind of information do you need?" she asked.

"Do you know anything about what happened to the guys that raped us?"

Logan was silent. She did not say anything for a while.

"Logan. Are you still there?"

"Sam, I really don't want to get involved in this."

"I'm not sure what you are referring to? What happened? I promise all you have to do is tell us what happened and we won't bother you anymore. We really just want to know so that when we come home, we don't have to be scared for our life."

"You won't be."

"What do you mean Logan?" said Lil. "I have nothing to say to you, Lil – not after you gonna threaten me. Sam, I will talk to you only. Please take me off speaker."

I picked up the phone and Logan explained to me that the big burly guy, the slim guy, the light-skinned guy, and Melvin were all dead. She said that her brother told her that Ron and Michael showed up on the strip with some guys in business suits. They all had guns. Her brother said that Michael, Ron, and the other guys in business suits knew exactly who they were going after. It was four guys in business suits. Each of them took a shot.

Michael shot Melvin execution style in the head. Then, Ron shot the big burly guy. Out of the four guys with business suits remaining, one of them shot the light-skinned guy and the other shot skinny guy, all execution style in the head. The two remaining guys had guns to the head of the dealers who were on the strip and threatened them to keep their mouth shut. The shootings all happened simultaneously.

I asked Logan how did her brother know that it was Ron and Michael. Logan told me that she asked the same question and that her brother told her that only one person other than her brother knew and that was one of the guys that were instructed not to tell. He recognized Michael from back in the day when he used to run the streets. Nobody else knows it was Michael and Ron. Logan said her brother promised her that nothing else would be heard of those guys. I was shocked. Lil was watching me intently since I no longer had the phone on speaker. She could not hear, but she knew that there was something wrong just by looking at the expression on my face. She sat there quietly and waited until I got off the phone with Logan. Before I ended the call, Logan and I promised to stay in touch. Then we said our goodbyes and I thanked her for all her help.

Before I could hit end on my cell phone, Lil started with her questions, drilling me by asking what Logan had said. Before I could get one question answered, she was asking me another one. I told her to take a breath and to have a seat because she was going to need all the strength she had to avoid passing out due to anxiety. I told her that Michael and Ron killed the guys that raped us.

Lil started screaming, "Oh no! Oh no!"

I told her to stay calm and lower her voice so that no one would hear her. Lil got up from my bed and sat on the floor with her head between her legs. I asked her if she was ready for me to continue. She told me yes. I told her that Ron and Michael and some guys in business suits shot the rapists point blank in the head. Lil was asking for all the details now. I told her exactly as Logan told me. I told her about the guys in the business suits and how each one executed one guy. I told her about the two that threatened the dealers not to snitch and how one of them knew Michael from back in the day. I also told her that Logan's brother said that although the murders happened with other folks around, nobody else knows them and nobody would snitch anyway for fear of their life.

After I finished telling Lil all I knew from what Logan shared, I sat down next to her on the floor, grabbed Lil's hands and asked her how do we handle the information we just got? Lil said we had to act as if we didn't know and never ever bring it up to Ron or Michael or tell them that we know what happened. She also suggested that we work on saving our marriage and family. She was right. Also, the fact that our husbands took care of the guys who caused harm to us was a sure sign that they were not going to leave us. We vowed to complete the remaining weeks we had, and then go back home and fight for our family.

CHAPTER 21

It was the last day of the treatment program, and Lil and I completed it successfully. Ron and Michael had just arrived at the airport and were on their way to pick us up. I never wanted to see that place again. It served as a reminder of all the things I did wrong in my life. I hugged my therapist and thanked her for all of her help. She told me that I was going to be fine and that I had nothing to worry about. She said she saw in me that I had pride and that most people with pride don't stay on drugs long.

Believe it or not, she was right. I was too proud to be seen as a drug abuser, and I did not want that title. It is embarrassing to have people know that I had a drug problem and needed to be entered into a program.

Let's be real, when people find out you are or were a drug addict, they treat you different.

It's sad but true. I was actually one of the people who would turn my nose up at drug addicts, especially with my sister Marie. I hate to admit it now, but I treated her like she was less than because of her habit. I could not understand how she could leave her kids for our sister Debra to care for while she is out on the streets. Wow, God has a way of making you see the light. There I was judging her and now here I am recovering from being a crack addict. God also has a sense of humor because the funny thing about it is that I tried crack because of Marie. Now that I am clean and practicing self-love, that was the stupidest thing I have ever heard of. I am really embarrassed to share that story, but as I've learned as part of treatment, sharing my story is a part of my healing and staying clean. So, I have prepared myself for the snickering or giggles that will happen when I share with other recovering addicts that I tried crack for weight loss.

When Ron and Michael arrived, they packed the SUV that they had rented with our things, said goodbye to the Therapists and we were on our way home. They appeared genuinely happy to see us. Lil and I had to do our best to act normal and not show any emotion about what we know about what they did. Last night, it really sank in for me. My husband is a murderer. I don't know how I feel about that. On one hand, I'm glad he took care of those bastards. They were trying to kill Lil and me, and we should have taken them out when we had the chance. Plus, it felt good that my husband protected me. I felt bad that four lives were lost. However, when I think about what they've done to other women and the destruction they'd caused to their lives as well as mine, I'm not that sorrowful. I know Ron and Michael used to run the streets together back in the day before we even met. It seemed as though they still had some connections and were still bad ass.

During the flight back home, we were seated in first class. I had a cranberry juice and reclined my seat to ease some of the tension I felt. Ron and Michael had a few drinks. Lil ordered an orange juice and read her magazine. I'm sure she was feeling the anxiety of going back home as well. The kids were due home in two weeks. Ron said that neither he nor Michael told the kids anything about where we were and what happened to us. All I know at this very moment is that I needed to get home and get my home and life together to prepare for them so that they don't feel any discomfort. Kids have the amazing ability to pick up on things when there is something wrong and you are trying your best to make it seem like everything is fine. That is what I need to determine, how Ron and I are going to exist in our home prior to Ronda and Sam coming home. I know he is not ready to be intimate with me but I need to know how long he will need to feel that I am worthy. I felt as though he was punishing me for being raped.

When the plane landed, we took the tram to the parking area, loaded Michael's car with our luggage and headed home. Michael and Lil dropped Ron and me off at our home and then headed to their house. When I arrived home, I felt like a stranger. As I walked in from the garage, I just stood in the kitchen area and looked around. I could not believe that I am at risk of losing all of this. This house holds all of my most precious memories. As I stood there, all of the memories of us purchasing the home, conceiving both kids, raising the kids, Christmas dinner, card parties, and Lil and me binging on the couch with a pint of ice cream because we were depressed about our weight. I sure would give anything to be back to those days where the worry over gaining a little weight and what I was cooking for Christmas was all I had to deal with. I have complicated my life to such an extent that I'm not sure how to go about repairing it.

I must have been standing in the kitchen area for a while because Ron walked up to me and told me that it would be ok. I didn't realize I was in tears. I just got lost in the memories. He hugged me and gently kissed my forehead. He told me that we have a lot of repairing to do with our marriage but he would do his best to work on it. He said that right now, the only thing that mattered is the kids and ensuring that they come back to a normal household. We unpacked and went back to our normal routine. He took our bags upstairs, and I looked in the fridge to see what was in there for me to cook. Most of the items in the fridge had expired, so I began tossing things out. I made a personal note to go to the grocery store in the morning. I looked in the freezer and saw a pack of salmon. Perfect, I thought. I would fix that with some brown rice and the Brussel sprouts that were also in the freezer. It would not take long to prepare.

I pulled out some salmon marinade that I had in the cabinet, placed the salmon in a freezer bag, and then poured the marinade over the salmon and placed it in the fridge. I cut the Brussel sprouts in half, put them in a freezer bag, sprinkled them with sea salt and olive oil, and put them in the fridge. Next, was the brown rice. I put chicken stock in a sauce pan and brought it to boil, added the rice and turned the heat down to simmer. That all took about forty minutes. I really did not have to cook anything today, but I needed something to do, and I used cooking as an excuse to avoid going upstairs to face Ron. I just didn't know what to say or how to act since I had put him in this awkward situation. I prayed that God would give me guidance and answers on how I should proceed.

Ron and I ate dinner in total silence. That is the first time in our entire marriage where we sat at the table together and did not say a word. I wanted to talk, but the expression on Ron's face told me that it was not the time and to leave him alone. After he finished eating his dinner, he quietly got up, placed his dishes in the sink, and went upstairs to our bedroom. I wanted to go up there to take a shower but I'm not sure how to handle it. I decided to go up into our bedroom anyway. I washed the dishes and put them away after drying them. I was a little perturbed because Ron had just said to me that it was going to take time and he kissed me on my forehead. Now he has no words for me. I don't no what is going on.

Once the dishes were all put away, I hesitantly headed upstairs to our bedroom. When Ron saw me come in, he got up and left. The way he looked at me was with distaste. I knew then that I would sleep in the guest room and give him his space. I grabbed me some PJs, panties, bras, and some outfits that would last me a week and went into the guest room. I took me a hot shower and released all of the pinned up anger I had been withholding. As the tears rolled down my eyes, the shower water washed them away. I stayed in the shower for about two hours. After I was done showering and crying, I was exhausted. I put on my PJs and went to sleep.

When I woke up the next morning, Ron was already gone. I called Lil from my cell and asked her how her evening was. She said that Michael was talking about a separation. She said they talked last night and right now he can't get over her cheating on him with Melvin. I told Lil about how Ron acted and how he did not have anything to say to me and how he did not want to be in the same room with me. I told her that I just don't understand the 360-degree attitude change. Lil filled me in on what Michael had told her. He and Ron agreed to be there for us while we were in the treatment facility. After that, they would deal with their real feelings.

Apparently, Michael's real feelings was a separation right now. It appeared that Ron may be leaning in that direction as well. I told Lil that I just didn't get it. Why would they commit murder for us, and then treat us like trash? I felt worse now than when I was at the treatment facility. Lil said that to top it off, Michael still wants the HIV test done and that she was headed to the doctor in a few minutes to get it done.

Since Lil and I have the same OB/GYN, I called him to see if I could get an appointment as well, and he was able to squeeze me in. I called Lil back and told her that I would meet her there. Lil's appointment was at 11:00 and my appointment was at 11:30. When the doctor called me in, I explained to him that I wanted to have an

HIV test done and that if he could rush getting the results, I would greatly appreciate it. The doctor recommended that I take the HIV antigen/antibody test instead of just the HIV antibody test by itself because it can detect both HIV antigen and HIV antibodies in the blood. An antigen/antibody test can detect HIV infection before an HIV antibody test. He told me that it usually takes 3-10 days to get the results. He also said that if the test comes out with a positive result, it would be retested to confirm the result, and that is when I would be notified. I asked him that if it comes back in three days, then it is good. However, if it takes longer should I be worried. He told me not to worry and that he has been my doctor for fifteen years and that I had nothing to worry about. I told him ok but made a mental note that he did not answer my question.

Lil was waiting for me when I came out of the doctor's office. We left and stopped at the Thai Restaurant for lunch. Lil ordered Pad Thai and a glass of red wine. I ordered the Drunken Noodles and also got a glass of wine. We couldn't believe that our husbands wanted us to take an HIV test. They all wore a condom and it was over so quick that the condom didn't have time to break. We just laughed and said that we were going to go through the motions just to shut them up. We started talking about back-to- school shopping for the kids. We knew we had to wait until we see them next week because we know that they probably have gotten big. That was another topic, we wondered if Ron and Michael would want us to go get the kids or whether they were planning to go with us. I told Lil that I would leave a note for Ron and ask him that question. We both started laughing. This was so crazy. We thought we would be great once we got out of the treatment facility.

However, now we are realizing that the hard part is just beginning.

Once I got home from the doctor and lunch with Lil, Ron was in the family room watching television. I felt strange walking in the house and not speaking. My mother raised me to always speak when entering a room. I said hello to Ron.

He responded, "Don't forget that you need to take the HIV test."

"I didn't forget. I took the test today. The results can take up to ten days."

"Oh, I'm surprised you went to take it. You must be worried that you contracted something."

I raised my voice, "Ron, I am not worried. The guys used a

condom. You asked for the test, so I got the test done! Why are you making me feel guilty for getting raped? You think I wanted it to happen?"

Ron was now yelling back at me.

"I don't think you wanted it to happen, but it wouldn't have happened if you had not been so stupid and tried crack to try and lose some fucking weight!"

"Oh! And there it is! That is the reason for your attitude. Why were you acting as if everything was ok at the treatment facility?"

"I decided to support you while you were getting help and deal with the real issues when you got home. I'm still fucking pissed. How can you be so naïve, Sam? You are such a smart lady. That is one of the things that attracted me to you. You want to know the other thing that attracted me to you? Your size! I liked you the size you were. I never asked you to lose weight to please me. I was well pleased. Then, you went and ruined everything!"

"I'm sorry, Ron."

That was all I could say at that moment. He got up and headed up the stairs. Before he made it to the top of the stairs, I yelled up at him and asked him how were the kids getting home next weekend. He yelled back and said he took care of it, and it does not include my involvement. He said that they will see me when they get home. I was pissed.

"You are not going to keep my kids away from me, Ron! You can be angry and I understand your anger, but I will be damned if I let you turn my kids against me."

"I'm not going to turn your kids against you. What the hell kinda of person do you think I am. I am pissed at you, and I really can't tell you where we will be as far as our relationship. However, that has nothing to do with our children. I'm trying Sam and you have to give me time"

"Take all the time you want Ron, but I only ask that you respect me. I already feel bad and your insults don't help me."

He didn't respond and walked into the master bedroom and closed the door. For the next three days it was like that. No conversation and when I come into the room he goes out of it or in the other direction. It had been five days and I have not heard anything back from the Doctor about my HIV status. I called Lil and asked her if she has heard anything. She said she had not heard anything either. They were probably just slow. I was expecting to hear something back in three days because I am pretty sure I am negative.

Lil mentioned that Michael moved out. She said he didn't take any furniture and said that he would have his attorney to draw up the separation papers. He would continue to pay the mortgage. He requested a six-month separation. When that is over, they would evaluate and determine whether they were going to stay married or get a divorce. Lil sounded more like she was angry instead of hurt. She called him a coward. Now that I think of it, Lil was using the anger to hide the hurt. She asked me to meet her to ride with her to the grocery store because she needed to get groceries in the house for the kids' arrival next week. I needed to get some groceries too, so I told Lil that I would meet her there. She said no and that she would swing by to get me because she needed the company, so she didn't want me to meet her there. I agreed and Lil was at my house in five minutes.

As I left the house, Ron was in the family room. He didn't say a word. Once I hopped in Lil's car and we began backing out of the driveway, I saw the blinds in the family room open, Ron was looking to see who picked me up. It was funny, he wanted to see who I was leaving with but he can't part his lips to speak to me. Lil and I had her car filled up where it was hard to see out the back windows. I put all of my groceries on the right side and she put her groceries on the left side. We had an umbrella in the center separating her stuff from mine. When we pulled up to my house, she helped me take the bags in. Ron was nowhere in sight, but he was home. He didn't even come down to help bring the groceries in.

Once Lil left and I was putting away the groceries, Ron came into the kitchen. He told me that the doctor's office called and wanted me to call them. Ron had the phone in his hand and wanted me to call the doctor right then and put it on speaker. I looked at him and told him that I would call the doctor when I was ready not because he wanted me to. He went into a rant and told me that I was hiding something. I told him that I had nothing to hide. That is when he handed me the phone and said prove it. I dialed the doctor's number and the receptionist answered. I told her that I was returning the doctor's call. She put me on hold and about two minutes later, the doctor came on the phone. He told me that he needed me to come in and discuss my results. My heart started beating. I was sweating like crazy. He asked if I could be there in thirty minutes. I could not respond. Ron chimed in and said that we would be there. The doctor spoke to Ron and said he would see us shortly.

I didn't say a word on the drive to the doctor's office. Ron insisted that he drive because he saw that I was nervous. He asked me if there was anything else that I needed to tell him. I said no and that I had told him everything. He had a look of uncertainty on his face. Once we arrived at the doctor's office, we were immediately taken back to see the doctor. He instructed us to have a seat. He took a deep breath and then delivered the news:

"Samantha, I'm sorry to report this news to you, but we ran your test three times and each time it came back positive. You are HIV positive."

Ron jumped up. No way! How could that be? I was in total shock. I did not expect for my test to come back as positive. The doctor asked me questions. He said he know there is something that I am not telling him and that he needed to know. Ron chimed in and told the doctor that I was raped. The doctor said that made sense on why I wanted a test out of the blue. I told him that they used condoms. The doctor asked what did I mean by they. Ron chimed in again and told him that three men raped me. The doctor asked if I reported it to the police. Ron told the doctor that there was no need to. He and the doctor made eye contact, and it seemed as though the doctor knew exactly what Ron was saying. He then began to ask me about my dealings with them and as I explained to him what happened to me, I remembered a major detail that I did not tell Ron about. Melvin had us drugged with a syringe needle! That is probably how I contracted the infection. If Lil tests positive, then I am more than likely right.

Ron was so angry, and he was holding his composure at the doctor's office. Especially when the doctor took his blood for him to be tested. That humiliated him. When we got home, he went in on me and said things to me that my worst enemy would never said to me. I tried to explain to him that I simply didn't remember about the needles because I was so traumatized about being gang banged. All he was concerned about was that he had better not have HIV. He told me that if he had it, I was dead, and I actually believed him. Actually, my death at that moment would have been a blessing. I didn't want to face this situation.

As soon as Ron left the house, I called Lil. She was crying. She had gotten her results back earlier in the morning and had to take Michael in with her to get tested. Her test was positive as well. Lil said that Michael humiliated her. She said that she could never ever be with him again. Although he doesn't want her, she just could not believe the things he said to her. When I explained to her how I think we contracted the HIV, Lil was in agreement. She was sure that was how we got it as well. From that day forward, our lives would never ever be the same.

CHAPTER 22

Ron stopped communicating with me. He got his test results back, and they were negative. He informed me that he was moving out and that he would continue to pay the mortgage until the divorce was final. I was shocked to hear him say divorce. He told me that he could not be married to someone who had HIV because of a stupid decision of trying crack. He did not want to risk his health nor his children's health. He said that he would let me stay in the house until the court made the decision of how to split the profits. He told me that the kids would be living with him until I learned how to live with HIV to ensure that his kids were not at risk of contracting the disease. He wanted me to stay away from the kids for one month to get myself together and allow him time to explain it to them. I lost it! I told him there was no way he was going to keep me from my kids. He could have the divorce, and I wouldn't contest it.

However, he would pay dearly for it. How dare he make me out to be the enemy when I was the one that was hurt, abused, and used. I was angry now.

I told him, "Yeah, I am fucked for trying crack. I got addicted to it, Ron, but I am no different from anyone else who made a mistake.

You fucking think I went out here to get raped, drugged, and to contract HIV. You are a stupid motherfucker. You are fucking blaming me. Get the fuck out of here, now!"

I went into the room and began throwing his things out the front door. He was pissed. He grabbed my arm and threw me to the floor.

He then got on top of me and put his hands around my neck. He was choking me so hard. I was struggling trying to get away. I began to lose consciousness. He let go, and I started gasping for air. He got up, grabbed his keys, picked up his clothes off the front lawn and drove away. I called Lil sobbing hysterically. I was trying to tell her what happened, but I could not get to the point where she could understand me. She told me that she was on her way, and then she hung up. The front door was unlocked and Lil walked in. It seemed like she got to my house in less than two minutes.

I was laying on the couch in the family room. She came over to me and I explained to her what happened. Lil was surprised that Ron acted in that manner. That was more of Michael's reaction. Lil calmed me down. She said that she spoke with an attorney and explained to him what happened. The attorney said that she would have a hard time getting any property or assets because of her infidelity. She told me that I had a good case because she showed how Ron blamed me for being raped even though I made a mistake. Lil told me that we had to deal with our diagnosis and fight for our life. We already had thugs try to take it away, there was no way we would let our husbands take it. She also reminded me that we had a card to use if they got stupid.

Ron and Michael went to pick up the kids from my parents' house. Michael followed Ron's lead and decided to not let Lil see her kids for a month as well. There we were, back to where we started, alone with no kids or husbands. The only difference was that no crack would be smoked. Although I'm smaller and actually at the size eight I always desired, it was not all it was cracked up to be. I looked better with the voluptuous body and curves that I had before the crack diet. Lil pulled out a bottle of wine and I used my laptop to go online to research how to live with HIV. The information on the web explained that with the advance in medicine, many people live a long happy life. It gave the advice to eat healthy, exercise, and stay happy.

It also had information advising that one should not be depressed or have major stress in their life. It said stress and depression are triggers to make your immune system go haywire and you will get really sick. It also said that if you have HIV, you need to inform people you are close to. We discussed having the conversation with our children. I told her that I was going to let them know that I was raped and that I wasn't sure if I wanted to tell them about me using crack. Lil explained that she really didn't have a choice because Michael would tell them everything. She said because Michael is so hurt, he was trying to do anything to hurt her. She said that after his test came back negative, he got even worse.

We decided that we were going to have to survive this together. Amazingly enough, we were not in tears or distraught. We had been through so much over the last three months and we both feel numb. At this point, nothing can hurt us. The damage is already done. If only we knew how beautiful we were at the time and loved the women we saw in the mirror, we would not have thought it was a great idea to try crack to lose weight. We were damaged about our body image as children, and we never had any therapy to manage those demons within that constantly told us we were not accepted by society because of the extra pounds we carried. If I had that therapy, I would not have felt less than at Ron's company parties or cookouts. I would have put on a bathing suit at the beach instead of shorts and a t-shirt. I also would have cherished memories with my kids because I would have gotten in the water instead of sitting on the lounge chair, watching them, and waving at them as they begged me to get in the water. I would have attended more events. Instead, I stayed home because I didn't want people to comment about my weight.

As I look back over my life, I realize that I didn't really live. I hid from life all because of my weight. I'm in so much pain. I snapped out of the state of sorrow I was in and looked over at Lil who seemed to be at a very low place. She wasn't listening to me as I read the article on the web of how to live with HIV. I called her name, and she jumped.

"You ok, Lil?"

"Not really Sam, but I will be fine. I will take care of me."

"Yes, we have to take care of each other.

That is the only way we will survive." "Yeah, I know Sam."

Lil seemed so low. I accepted the fact that I would have to be the strong one to get us through this. I hugged her and kissed her forehead. She hugged me back and told me that she loved me. She said that she needed to get back to the house. I asked her to spend the night here, and we would stay at her house tomorrow. She agreed and said that she needed to go home and get some clothes. I told her that she had clothes upstairs, she said that she needed some other things as well. I told her to be back in an hour so that we could watch a movie and order a pizza. She agreed and left. I had a sneaky suspicion that she wanted to leave so she could smoke some crack. She was acting weird, and it seemed as though she really didn't want to stay the night with me. I made a note that if she was not here in an hour, I was going to pop up at her house. I still had my spare key so she would not expect me.

An hour and a half had passed and I had not heard from Lil. I called her home phone and she did not answer the phone. I called her cell phone and she did not answer that either. I called continuously, rotating between the cell and the home phones and she did not answer. It was now two hours later. I picked up my keys, located the spare key to Lil's house and headed there. Her car was in the driveway when I pulled up. She must have been in there smoking crack.

I used my key to enter through the front door. Once I was in, I called her name.

"Lil. Where are you? You were supposed to be at my house two hours ago."

Lil did not answer. I immediately went downstairs to the room where we smoked crack at. She was not there. I continued to call her name. She didn't answer. I started thinking that maybe she went somewhere with someone else. I headed upstairs. I checked the kitchen, family room, living room, and the laundry room. There was no sign of Lil. I then went upstairs to the bedroom level. I checked the kids room and their bathrooms. I thought maybe she would be in there because she missed her kids. She was not there. I checked the guest room and that bathroom. She was not there. I checked the Master bedroom, and when I walked in, I saw Lil in the bed. As I approached her, I saw blood running down her face. There was a huge hole in her face!

There was a gun lying next to her and a note on the pillow. I was unable to stand. I screamed and screamed. I was devastated and could not believe that she would leave me.

However, I also had a calm sense of understanding. I, too, had thought about leaving this world. However, Lil, my husband, and my kids were the reasons why I decided not to do it. That has changed now. Lil's note read:

"I have made a mistake in my life. Because of that mistake, my life has changed forever. That is not acceptable to me. Goodbye."

As I read the note, I kept saying you can't leave me. I had to make the decision on whether to call the police. I did not want to have to tell the story again of what happened. Also, I was thinking that what if the gun Lil used was from the murders that Michael committed. What would happen with her kids? I had to take matters into my own hands. I grabbed the gun from the bed. I took off my shoes and crawled up in the bed next to Lil. I hugged her, kissed her, and told her that I loved her. I said a long prayer to God and asked for his forgiveness for what I was getting ready to do. Then, I grabbed my cell phone and opened up the recorder app and began recording my last words:

"To my husband, I'm sorry I hurt you.

Please know that all I've done was in an effort to keep you happy and interested in me. I made a huge mistake, and I'm sorry. Because of my mistake, I have to face something for the rest of my life that I am not willing to face. Please do not tell our children about what I did and what I contracted. I don't want them to know any of this. I hope you are happy now, Ron. You blamed me for being raped, and you never thought of the pain I had to endure. The last straw was being diagnosed with HIV. I can't bear to live my life like that. So, you see Ron… Yes, trying crack was a stupid fucking idea and guess what - I paid the price. I just wish I had your support to help me feel, worthy but since I don't, there is no way I can go it alone. You see I didn't plan to end my life. Lil and I were supposed to watch a movie. When I went to check on her. I found her in her bed with a bullet hole in her head. Now, I have no one. I can't live without her. She left a letter on the pillow. I'm sure the police will show it to you and Michael.

Thanks to the both of you for the lack of support. Please tell my family that I love them, and I'm sorry. Goodbye. P.S. Don't cry for me."

I kept the recorder playing because I wanted Ron to hear when I pulled that trigger. I know it was wrong, but as I made that recording, I began to get really consumed with anger and all I wanted was for him to suffer. As long as he doesn't share the recording with my kids, all is fine. They are innocent and have nothing to do with this. On the contrary, he should feel the guilt that I'm feeling, because he had no interest or empathy in trying to understand my pain. Well, I'm going to give him a new level of pain, and maybe he would then understand. It's sad that it had to get to this level. My best friend was gone, and I was on my way to join her. I slowly took the gun that Lil used to end her life, placed it up to my right temple, and pulled the trigger.

The Nibor Group, LLC Reading Group Guide

"All Cracked Up came about when a girlfriend and I were discussing a relative who was on crack cocaine. We jokingly said that if crack makes you lose weight like that, we should try it. That prompted me to think that it would make a good book. Twenty years later, I wrote the book." - Madison Love

Madison Love's mission is to empower women to love themselves. Unfortunately, many women make unwise decisions based on a lack of self-love. As in this book, Sam and Lil did not love themselves enough.

Their self-esteem was damaged at an early age, and they didn't have anyone to tell them how beautiful, smart, and wonderful they naturally were. Many women are in situations today because they fill inadequate. So I challenge every woman reading this book to look in the mirror and love what you see! Self-Love to all!

QUESTION FOR DISCUSSION

1. What are your thoughts on the relationship between Sam and Lil? Do you share that close bond with a friend?

2. How did you feel about Samantha (Sam) and Lily's (Lil) decision to try crack? Do you think in the real world that someone would really try crack to lose weight?

3. Who did you relate to the most, Sam or Lil?

4. Did you feel that things were going to start going downhill when Sam and Lil forget to pick the kids up from camp?

5. How did the incident with Sam's boss Daniel impact you?

6. Do you think Daniel got what he deserved?

7. What is your opinion of Logan?

8. Do you think she should have stood up for herself and not let Daniel abuse her?

9. Do you agree with Sam's reaction to how her boss talked to her?

10. How were you impacted with the rape of Sam and Lil?

11. Did you have any reaction to the light- skinned guy mentioning his mom while raping Sam?

12. Do you think that Sam and Lil should have killed their rapists when they escaped?

13. Do you agree with how Ron and Michael reacted once they found out that Sam and Lil were raped?

14. Do you think they were insensitive?

15. Do you agree with Ron and Michael murdering the guys who raped their wives? If you don't agree, do you think it was justifiable?

16. Were you surprised that Sam and Lil were diagnosed with HIV?

17. Did you forget that they were drugged by being injected with a syringe needle before being rape? This was a major detail that both Sam and Lil forgot about which was the cause of their diagnosis.

18. If you were Ron or Michael, would you stay in the marriage knowing that your spouse was diagnosed with HIV?

19. Were you surprised by the ending?

20. What was the most disturbing part in the book for you?

21. What do you believe the major objective of this book is?

www.ingramcontent.com/pod-product-compliance
Lightning Source LLC
Chambersburg PA
CBHW071247130626
46556CB00003B/1199